Mason wanted [her, but did] he want her as [much as she] wanted him?

Charlene wasn't sure. [The] truth waited on the other side of the door, and she just didn't know if she could face it yet. Sinking onto the porch swing, she picked up a box of Mint Crème cookies. Five percent mint and ninety-five percent chocolate, which put them near the top of her Hands Off list.

Right beneath Mason McGraw, who'd occupied the top spot for as long as she could remember.

The thought stirred an image of him naked and panting over her, surrounding her, inside her…

She opened the box and dived in. She was on her sixth cookie when she heard the front door open.

"Those must be some cookies." Mason pulled the door closed and stepped towards her.

"They're all right," Charlene said after swallowing a mouthful and trying to calm her frantic heart. "Want a taste?" she said, holding the box out to him.

"I definitely want a taste." Then he took the box and set them aside. Before she knew what was happening, he'd dropped to his knees in front of her and was reaching for the waistband of her skirt.

"What are you doing?"

"Helping myself," he murmured as he tugged her zip down…

Dear Reader,

I would love to say that I was the coolest/prettiest/most popular girl in school, but exactly the opposite was true. I wore braces for six years, had what I like to refer to as a bad-hair "decade" and was voted (get ready to gag) Most Studious. I look back now and I'm extremely proud that my classmates recognised my smarts. But at the time, I might as well have had a great big G branded on my forehead (for Geek, of course). Like most other girls, I secretly dreamed of wearing the trendiest clothes and dating the captain of the football team.
Deep sigh…

The heroine in my newest Blaze novel is no different. Charlene Singer is queen of the Late Bloomers. In school she was awkward and geeky and practically invisible to the cool kids, including Mason McGraw, the hunkiest cowboy to ever saddle up a horse. But that didn't stop her from fantasising.

Little does she know, but Mason spent his youth nursing a few erotic thoughts of his own. And when he returns to Romeo, Texas, to take over his family's ranch and reclaim his home, he's got more than just horse wrangling on his mind. Sexy, sophisticated Charlene is just what Mason needs for his own happily ever after, and he intends to prove it to her. The temperature isn't the only thing that gets hot down in Texas when these two join forces to breathe life into their most erotic daydreams.

I hope you enjoy my latest Blaze book featuring the McGraw brothers! I love to hear from readers. You can visit me online at www.kimberlyraye.com

Much love from deep in the heart!

Kimberly Raye

TEXAS FIRE

BY
KIMBERLY RAYE

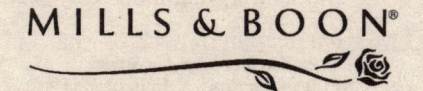

MILLS & BOON®

This book is dedicated to Late Bloomers everywhere.
We make the world go 'round, ladies!

DID YOU PURCHASE THIS BOOK WITHOUT A COVER?
If you did, you should be aware it is **stolen property** as it was reported *unsold and destroyed* by a retailer. Neither the author nor the publisher has received any payment for this book.

All the characters in this book have no existence outside the imagination of the author, and have no relation whatsoever to anyone bearing the same name or names. They are not even distantly inspired by any individual known or unknown to the author, and all the incidents are pure invention.

All Rights Reserved including the right of reproduction in whole or in part in any form. This edition is published by arrangement with Harlequin Enterprises II B.V. The text of this publication or any part thereof may not be reproduced or transmitted in any form or by any means, electronic or mechanical, including photocopying, recording, storage in an information retrieval system, or otherwise, without the written permission of the publisher.

This book is sold subject to the condition that it shall not, by way of trade or otherwise, be lent, resold, hired out or otherwise circulated without the prior consent of the publisher in any form of binding or cover other than that in which it is published and without a similar condition including this condition being imposed on the subsequent purchaser.

MILLS & BOON and MILLS & BOON with the Rose Device are registered trademarks of the publisher.

*First published in Great Britain 2006
by Harlequin Mills & Boon Limited, Eton House,
18-24 Paradise Road,
Richmond, Surrey TW9 1SR*

© Kimberly Raye Groff 2005

ISBN-13: 978 0 263 84614 0
ISBN-10: 0 263 84614 8

14-0906

*Printed and bound in Spain
by Litografia Rosés S.A., Barcelona*

1

CHARLENE SINGER STOOD near the rear exit of the Elks Lodge, stared at the man leaning against the bumper of the black 4x4 pickup truck directly in her line of escape and wished with all of her heart that she believed in alien abductions.

She needed a quick escape.

Her day—okay, make that her *month*—was quickly going from bad to worse. It had started when the queen of the gourmet sex desserts had moved to town and started poisoning the good women of Romeo with the insane theory that the way to a man's heart was through his senses. To add insult to injury, the women actually *believed* such nonsense. Miss Sweet & Sinful had just preached her message to a lodge full of Juliets— Romeo's local women's club—and had received a standing ovation. The Juliets had practically fallen over themselves to get to the table of hand-outs detailing several explicit recipes for sexual success. Sex. As if that were a solid basis for any long-term relationship. Feed him this and tease him with that, and he'll fall hook, line and sinker from this day forward, 'til death do us part.

Yeah, right.

Charlene folded the tip sheet she'd swiped and stuffed it into the pocket of her slim-fit beige skirt. The Juliets had been too enthralled by the advice to notice that Dr. Charlene Singer, Romeo's one and only relationship therapist, had actually attended one of their self-help luncheons. Talk about fuel for Skeeter McBee and his gossip circle down at the diner.

Romeo was the typical small Texas town. And like any typical small Texas town diner, the Fat Cow Café had become notorious for its platter-sized chicken fried steak smothered in cream gravy, served up with a generous side of homemade mashed potatoes and a great big scoop of "Didya hear? Willie McIntyre got caught wearing his wife's pantyhose…"

The ringleader of the gossip? Old Skeeter McBee, the reigning domino champ and leader of the lunch bunch—a handful of retirees who met every afternoon for the daily lunch special.

The Juliets were already questioning Charlene's doctrine. The last thing she needed was for someone to get the idea that she'd jumped ship and was now anxious to try out Miss Sweet & Sinful's recipes herself. Old Skeeter and his cronies would have a field day spreading that around.

Charlene had come strictly to size up the competition, and now she intended to make a nice, clean getaway before the meeting officially adjourned and someone singled her out.

Fat chance with her only available out—a beige Lexus she'd bought last year—parked several feet away. On the opposite side of the man and the truck.

From bad to worse to disastrous.

Charlene closed her eyes and fought down a wave of panic. There were only three things in life that made her truly miserable—chocolate, *The Bachelor* and Mason McGraw.

It wasn't the sweet, rich taste of chocolate that put everything dark, delicious and sinful at the top of her "unbearable things" list. She'd come closer to an orgasm with a bottle of YooHoo and a box of truffles than with most of the men she'd dated. It was the dreaded "morning after," as in zits, a face full of them that lasted longer than the dehydrated macaroni and cheese her mother had kept in their bad weather emergency kit, along with batteries, bottled water and multiple cans of Spam.

The Bachelor ranked in the top three because of its blatant objectification of women. Sure, there was a lot of blah-blah on the man's part about finding a soulmate with brains and ambition, and Charlene supposed there could be a thread of truth to it. What guy wanted to spend 'til death do us part with a dumb, lazy woman? But it wasn't an issue that any of the bachelors had yet to address. Thanks to the show's casting manager, brains and ambition came wrapped in a drop-dead gorgeous body, preferably with perky breasts, blond hair and a laser-bleached smile. So much for reality TV.

As for number three on the list…

Her gaze slid to the hot body in question. He'd obviously not heard the rear exit door creak open because his attention remained fixed on the front entrance of the lodge. An all-important fact which allowed her a few blessed moments to breathe, plan and study his profile.

Okay, so forget the breathing and planning. Mason McGraw had been back in Romeo all of two weeks and this was her first up-close look at him.

He wore faded Wranglers that molded to his long, lean legs and cupped the tush which rested on the front bumper of the jacked-up truck. Scuffed, tan Ropers hooked at the ankles, the toes scarred and worn from climbing into one too many saddles. His back rested against the massive silver grille, his arms folded. His biceps bulged, stretching the sleeves of his white T-shirt into a tight second skin and a beat-up straw Resistol sat low on his forehead. The brim curled down in the front and shielded his eyes from the blistering noonday sun, the straw edges ragged from years of handling. Dark hair curled out from under his hat and brushed the collar of his cotton T-shirt. The faintest hint of stubble darkened his strong jaw and circled his sensuous mouth. His Adam's apple bobbed and the muscles in his jaw tensed as he chewed at a piece of straw that hung from the corner of his mouth.

Dark, delicious and sinful… Check!

Mason still looked as tempting as the most decadent piece of Godiva, which wasn't a problem in and of itself. She'd eyeballed many a good-looking man. But he wasn't just handsome. He had this peel-off-your-clothes grin that made women want to strip now and think later—much later—and Charlene was no exception.

Not that she would sink so low as to hook up with a man who'd made no secret that he liked his women beautiful and dumb. But seeing that grin full-on... Well, it made her at least contemplate the notion for a full five seconds before coming to her senses and realizing that this was the same guy who'd paid a quarter back in the sixth grade to see Lolly Langtree's underpants.

Objectifies women... Check!

It hadn't mattered that Lolly had been as intelligent as a bag of rocks, and about as sensitive. She'd had a pretty face to go with her pretty pink *Charlie's Angels* panties, and so Mason had been the first in line when Lolly had stepped into the closet to give sneak peeks at Sandra Huckaby's first girl/boy party.

Meanwhile, Charlene had stood as far away as possible, not the least bit anxious to have anyone see the white cotton *Hee Haw* briefs her mom had bought on the clearance rack at the local K-Mart.

As if any of the boys would have given even a nickel to see them.

Charlene hadn't been one of the cool girls—daring divas as they'd called themselves back in junior high school—with their lip gloss and Calvin Klein jeans. Rather, she'd been the tallest girl in the class, and the most awkward. Her jeans—whatever brand that happened to be on sale at Sears or Montgomery Ward—had always been an inch too short for her body. Her one attempt at a tube of Lip Smackers had created enough of a glare—can you say Mick Jagger lips?—to temporarily blind the captain of the basketball team and screw up a winning three-pointer during the semifinals. At least that's what Sandra and Lolly and the other "divas" had said. To make matters worse, Charlene had worn thick glasses and battled monumental zits, and so she'd been snubbed for the most part like all of the other "groupies," also known as geeks.

While Charlene's own mother had been born a groupie—she'd been not only plain and geeky, but poor, as well—she'd managed to turn herself into a daring diva by marrying the mayor's son who'd gone on to become the president of Romeo Savings and Loan. And so Charlene had been invited to Sandra's party because their mothers had run in the same social set and played in the same bridge club. A humiliation in and of itself. Unfortunately, it had only been the first of many that night. Before the evening had ended, she'd become known to every kid at Romeo Junior High as Charlie Horse Underpants.

"Hey, there, Charlie Horse Underpants!"

"Here comes Charlie Horse Underpants!"

"How's it going, Charlie Horse Underpants?"

The memories echoed in her head and her throat tightened. The name didn't matter anymore. And it certainly didn't matter that Bobby Winchell down at the local Stop-n-Shop still said "Well, well, if it ain't Charlie Horse Underpants," every time she stopped off for a loaf of bread or a six-pack of Diet Coke.

Despite that some immature people still felt the need to tease her, she wasn't about to burst into tears anymore. She was all grown-up now and she realized that it wasn't about how a woman looked or what she wore that attracted a member of the opposite sex for the long-term. It was her inner being. Her personality.

Be yourself and men—the reliable, 'til death do us part, potential soulmate kind, that is—will flock to you.

That was her motto now, one she preached with complete conviction not only in her private practice as a relationship therapist, but also twice a week at nearby Texas A & M to an auditorium full of enthusiastic sociology majors. Forget the Boobs and Hair, It's All About Going Bare had become the college's most popular course, and had earned Charlene tenure just this past year.

Tenure, she reminded herself. When most of the other professors her age were still working on their thesis papers and building their credentials.

Charlene had already proven herself.

And her theory?

She'd seen the proof firsthand. Her parents, direct opposites, had had little in common, but they'd been attracted to each other anyway. They'd married, and they'd ended up in divorce court. The lust factor simply wasn't enough of a foundation for marriage. A couple needed common interests for that. Similar personalities. A meeting of the minds instead of the bodies. At least that's what Charlene had always believed, up until Miss Sweet & Sinful had come to town.

But after seeing the way the Juliets embraced the woman's preaching, Charlene couldn't help but wonder if Holly Farraday was on to something. Maybe a solid, lasting relationship wasn't built on common interests. Maybe it was just good sex.

And maybe not.

She didn't know. She only knew that she had to make a quick getaway because she wasn't going to risk her reputation on a *maybe*.

She drew a deep breath, gathered her courage and stepped forward. It wasn't like she had to actually walk in front of Mason. She could go around the rear of the truck and, thereby, avoid a confrontation. The first, in fact, since the night of Sandra Huckaby's party. Sure, she'd seen him since then. While he'd left town over sixteen years ago, right after high school graduation, he'd been back now and then for special occasions and, most recently, for his grandfather's funeral.

But in all the years since Sandra's party, Charlene had never actually talked to him.

She'd tried. The Monday after the underpants incident, she'd actually smiled at him in the hallway, but he'd simply stared past her. So she'd contented herself with lusting after him from afar and later, as she'd gotten older, in her most private fantasies.

It was a situation that suited her just fine. While she'd entertained erotic thoughts about Mason, he was as far from her soulmate as a man could get, and so she was in no hurry to run into him. Charlene wanted only one thing at this point in her life—to marry the right man, one who shared her interests, and to have a solid, lasting relationship.

She eyed her car. Okay, so maybe she wanted two things. A solid, lasting relationship, and a clean getaway.

The first wish was *this* close—she'd found the *man,* a colleague who shared her love of books and her passion for opera, and it was just a matter of time before he realized how perfect they were for each other. The second was close, as well, if only she could clear several yards of open space without making any—

Crrrrunch!

The sole of her Prada pump sank into the gravel and her breath caught.

Metal groaned and creaked. The pickup bobbed. More gravel crunched and crackled—sounds that had nothing to do with the tasteful, beige pumps she'd paid an obscene amount of money for during last month's shopping spree, and everything to do with worn boots and strong purposeful footsteps.

"Charlie?" The deep voice slid into her ears and sent a burst of heat through her.

Or maybe it was the sudden memory of her most embarrassing moment that did that.

Either way, she stiffened. Her head snapped to the side and she found herself staring into Mason's deep green eyes just the way she had that night when she'd accidentally left the bathroom door unlocked and he'd walked in on her. He'd had three boys trailing behind him and they'd all gotten a glimpse of her in her *Hee Haw* panties, her jeans down around her ankles.

But Mason had gotten the first look. The longest look…before the other boys had started laughing and calling her the name that would follow her all the way to her high school graduation and beyond.

"I see Paris, I see France. I see Charlie Horse Underpants!"

"Well, well, if it isn't Charlie—"

"I'm not wearing any underpants," Charlene blurted before he could say the rest of the dreaded name. "I mean, I *am* wearing underpants, but they're not the *Hee Haw* ones. I don't wear those anymore. I wouldn't have worn them *ever*, except my mother had this thing for buying me stuff on sale and I didn't exactly have a choice. But now I buy my own underwear and I usually stick to solid colors. No horses. Not that the *Hee Haw* ones even had horses. Technically, they were donkeys, but I guess Charlie Donkey didn't have the same ring to it."

Surprise registered in Mason's dark green gaze. He tipped the brim of his hat back, as if to get a better look at her. "That's good to know," he said.

And then he smiled.

No, forget the smile.

He *grinned,* his lips curving in that slow, sexy tilt that had made him the most sought after boy in Romeo even though he had two identical brothers just as wild and wicked and handsome.

She wasn't sure what she'd expected, but it certainly wasn't the deep, husky, "I'm a plaid man, myself."

The statement cut through her line of defense like a hot knife through butter and stirred an image of him wearing nothing but a pair of plaid boxers and a smile. Her mouth went dry and she licked her lips. "Well, I do have a pair with tiny hearts on them."

His grin widened. "Hearts are good."

Excitement rushed through her. A crazy reaction considering she could care less what he thought. She hadn't bought the hearts for him, or any man for that matter. She'd bought them because they hadn't had any solids in her size and cut and she'd simply felt like splurging. A compulsion that had grown from years of watching her mother budget and save and buy only marked-down merchandise. While her mother had transformed herself into a daring diva, she'd never quite escaped her past or the compulsion to hold on to her money.

Charlene could care less what Mason thought about her undies.

So why are you telling him?

To set the record straight. Because she'd never had a chance all those years ago because she'd never had the nerve to actually speak to him. And because she'd endured too many names all these years and she'd never once fought back. She'd never really had the courage. Until Mason McGraw had been about to say the hated name and she'd had to stop him.

That, and because she was having a major meltdown thanks to the legendary grin.

"I have a master's degree in behavioral science," she heard herself say. Okay, she was still blurting unsolicited information, but at least it had nothing to do with her underwear. "I teach a class at A & M on female empowerment. Not at this moment, mind you. We're on summer break, but the class is already full for this fall. I'm also a licensed relationship therapist. I have my own practice over near the courthouse."

"The white two-story colonial with the picket fence?" At her nod, he added, "Isn't that Dr. Connally's place?"

"I share the building with Stewart." That wasn't

all she wanted to share with him, if he would just realize that they were meant for each other.

Oddly enough, her lips seemed to tighten around that last bit of information.

"We're dating," she finally managed to say. "Sort of."

"How do you 'sort of' date someone?"

"Well, we have lunch once a week."

Mason let loose a low whistle. "Sounds serious."

"It will be. We've known each other since we were kids. We like the same things. It's just a matter of time."

"Congratulations," he said. Oddly enough, the sentiment didn't seem to touch his gaze. "Is that the Connally guy from sophomore chemistry? The one who burned his eyebrows off with the bunson burner?"

"They finally grew back." *After several special hair treatments in Austin.* "You can't even tell now."

"Good for him."

"So what about you? What have you, um, been up to?"

"I've been running my own ranch management consulting group, doing independent projects here and there. But now I'm home to take care of things at the Iron Horse."

"What does a ranch management consulting group do?"

"Ranches call me in to help modify their operation. I put them on a branding and breeding schedule, teach them the most effective ways to increase their herd size with their available resources. If they're a horse ranch, I do the same for their horses and also teach them the newest techniques in breeding and training," he said proudly.

"Who's going to run your business while you're home?"

"I sold half of the business to my chief manager. He's running things now and I'm just a silent partner."

"Sounds like you gave up a lot to come home." Charlene wondered if she'd have had the guts to do it. Probably not.

"Actually, I expect to gain a lot by coming home. My job has always kept me on the road and now I get to actually settle down in one place. No more living out of a suitcase."

"I guess that would be a plus."

Say goodbye, a voice whispered. *You've cleared the air, killed the teasing and done the small talk. Just excuse yourself, get into your car and leave. You don't want to know him. You don't want to like him. And you* don't *want the Juliets to see you.*

The sound of laughter drifted from the lodge entrance, signaling the dismissal of the meeting. Any minute, the doors would burst open and she'd be busted.

"Married?" she heard herself ask.

"Are you kidding?"

"Fiancée?"

"Hardly."

"Significant other?"

"Only a horse named Winston."

She couldn't help smiling. "So what are you doing here?"

"Josh is inside proposing right now." He indicated the souped-up GTO that sat just off to the side of the building. "So I thought I'd give him a little moral support."

"Moral support for a marriage proposal? And here I'd heard that the whole notion gave you the heebie jeebies."

"Actually, it does. And it used to have the same effect on my brother. Until he met this woman." He shrugged and glanced behind him at the entrance, a puzzled look on his face. As if he thought Josh was about to cut off his arm instead of pledging his life to a special woman.

"What's her name?"

"Holly Farraday," Mason said as his gaze collided with Charlene's. "She makes desserts and stuff."

"Ultimate Orgasms," Charlene clarified. "And Chocolate Body Bon Bons and Daring Divinity, and a dozen other things with suggestive names."

His eyebrows kicked up a notch. "Come again?"

"She makes aphrodisiac desserts that supposedly entice the senses and put a person in 'the mood.'"

Amusement glittered in his gaze. "Must be some damned powerful desserts."

"It's all propaganda to sell her product. Real attraction doesn't lie in the five senses. It goes deeper than that."

Mason eyed her. "Is that how it's going to be with you and Dr. Steven? When you start officially dating, that is?"

"His name's Stewart, and that's exactly how it's going to be. He won't need me flitting around, half-dressed, serving him glorified chocolate cake to make him feel frisky. Just talking with me will be enough for that."

"You sound pretty sure of yourself."

If only she felt half as sure.

"Stewart and I have a lot in common," she told him. "We don't need to worry about appealing to each other's senses."

"So why are you here?"

"Research purposes."

He arched an eyebrow before giving her another grin. "That's what they all say, sugar."

Her stomach fluttered and she stiffened. "I have to know what bunk is circulating in order to effectively debunk it. I'm sure Holly's desserts are delicious, but there's no way merely eating one can heighten the attraction between two people."

He gave her a wink. "Depends how you eat it."

The gleam in his eyes told her he wasn't talking about using plates or forks. Something sharp and sweet tickled between her legs and her breath caught.

"I..." She licked her lips and instantly regretted it when his gaze hooked on her mouth. Desire brightened his eyes.

Desire?

Because of some simple lip-licking?

Maybe on the most superficial level.

But Charlene didn't advocate superficial. She preached depth and commitment and destiny.

Besides, she didn't think for one second that Mason McGraw, *the* Mason McGraw, would actually lust after her. Sure, she'd changed. She wasn't the same gawky teenager she used to be. She wore better clothes and she'd conquered her raging acne. But she wasn't all that, either.

She wasn't nearly the daring diva she would have to be to interest Mason. Not that she wanted to interest him, mind you.

Charlene had long ago accepted who she was— serious, low-key and on the plain side—and she'd stopped pining away for bigger boobs, better hair and a more curvaceous figure. She simply wasn't meant to be bold, beautiful and big-breasted, and she wasn't meant to be with a man as good-looking as Mason. Oranges belonged with oranges and apples belonged with apples, as far as she was concerned.

That's the way it had been when she'd been young and the way it would always be. Despite the strange tension bubbling in the air between them.

"Here's my card," she told him, eager to distract

herself from the electricity skimming up and down her arms. She pulled the familiar piece of vellum from inside her purse and handed it to him.

"Excuse me?"

"In case you ever need any therapy."

She saw the twinkle in his gaze and she braced herself for the grin she knew would follow.

"Well, lookee what the cat dragged in." Lolly Langtree's voice killed Mason's expression and drew his attention.

A mix of relief and dread rolled through Charlene as she turned to see the blond, blue-eyed, once-upon-a-time captain of the Romeo cheerleading squad standing in the open double doorway.

"I was just—" Charlene started to say, but Lolly cut her off.

"If it isn't Mason McGraw," the woman declared as she stepped forward and made quick work of the gravel parking lot. Just like way back when, she didn't so much as spare Charlene a glance. "I'd heard you were back, but it's high time I saw for myself."

"Mason McGraw!" another voice shrieked as the double doors opened again and several more women spilled out into the parking lot.

"Ohmigod, it's Mason!" another voice squealed.

"What a sight for sore eyes."

"You're looking as good as ever!"

Charlene quickly found herself pushed aside as the women surrounded Mason.

She ignored the strange tightening in her chest the way she always had where Mason was concerned.

He wasn't her type. And she definitely wasn't his. Not then and not now.

She turned on her heel and headed for her car. Better to forget the real man wrapped up in his cotton T-shirt and skintight Wranglers and settle for her fantasies.

Better, but not easy, she realized as she caught herself chancing a glance behind her.

Not by a long shot.

2

MASON MCGRAW HAD TALKED orgasms with more than his share of women, but no such conversation had ever ended with a handshake and a business card.

"…surprise when I heard you were coming back for good…" Lolly's voice droned on, but the words didn't register.

Then again, this wasn't just any woman. This was Charlie Singer. Once upon a time, the smartest girl at Romeo High School, and the owner of the longest pair of legs.

His gaze followed her as she crunched across the gravel. She still had long legs, made even longer thanks to a pair of do-me high heels. But where she'd been somewhat awkward back then, she now moved with a smooth, fluid grace that came with maturity and, perhaps, a little practice. Her torso, which had once seemed immature and small for the rest of her, had broadened and filled out just enough to create an enticing silhouette and to balance her long limbs.

He zeroed in on the push-pull of fabric against her round ass. The soft material molded to her curves and swept the length of her legs to just below her knees. There was nothing remotely sexy about the blah beige skirt. If anything, it leaned toward the respectable side. Still, it stirred his curiosity and he couldn't help but wonder what lay beneath it. Smooth thighs and sweet curves and soft skin and… *Sex.*

His gaze went to the card she'd handed him.

Dr. Charlene Singer.

She was obviously still as smart as ever.

"If you ever need any therapy…"

Mason needed a lot of things at that moment, but therapy wasn't one of them.

He shifted his weight from one foot to the other, eager to give his damned dick a little breathing room.

Then again, he was hot and bothered over Charlie Horse Singer, for Christ's sake. Maybe he did need some therapy.

Charlie Horse.

The name echoed through his head, along with the memories of a painfully awkward girl who'd worn thick glasses and too-short jeans. She'd always stood off to the side, never participating. Just watching with her deep brown eyes. He'd never called her the name everyone else did. Hell, he'd never even talked to her. She hadn't been worth his effort when he'd had dozens of other girls to choose from—all prettier and more outgoing and not the least bit shy.

That's what he'd told himself back then, whenever he'd seen her at school or at the grocery store with her mom. She was Charlie *Horse,* and she wasn't worth a smile or a hello, or even a thought.

But Mason McGraw had thought about her anyway.

Fantasized about her.

From the moment he'd seen those long legs up close and personal, he hadn't been able to get her out of his head. Even more, he hadn't been able to forget the flicker of heat as he'd stared at her and she'd stared at him, her gaze as rich and tempting as his aunt's prize-winning chocolate cake. Everything else had faded away for a few seconds. There'd been no embarrassment. No awkwardness. No divas or groupies. Just the two of them and a fierce attraction.

An attraction he was free to act on now because Mason McGraw was home. For the first time in a long time, he was *home.*

While he'd been back over the years, he hadn't been able to settle down. He'd been busy with his business. And when his grandfather had been alive, the old man had constantly pushed him and his brothers away.

Not that his grandfather hadn't loved his triplet grandsons. He had. It's just that they'd been the spitting image of their father and reminded the elder McGraw daily of his loss.

When Mason and his brothers had been sixteen their mother had died from an unexpected miscarriage—she'd bled to death before anyone had realized what was happening. His father had been out cheating on her, as usual, and when the oldest of the triplets, Josh, had caught up with him, it had been too late for him to say goodbye. He'd been so guilt-stricken that he'd wrapped his car around a telephone pole in town and, in less than twenty-four hours, the McGraw triplets had lost both parents and their grandfather had lost his reason for living. He'd been so overcome with his grief that he'd pushed away any and all reminders of his son and daughter-in-law—namely his grandsons. The boys had all left home right after graduation and they'd been on the road ever since. While Mason's grandfather had eventually realized the error of his ways—he'd been diagnosed with prostate cancer a few years back and made peace with his grandsons before he died—things just hadn't been the same. Mason hadn't wanted to cause the old man any more stress, so he'd kept his distance, except for the occasional visit. But things were different now. Romeo McGraw was dead and Mason was home for good to fulfill the promise he'd made to his mother—to look after the land she'd loved with all of her heart. A love she'd shared with his father. That's all they'd shared, however.

Not a *real* attraction.

Not the kind that dug down deep in your gut and turned you inside out.

Not a bonafide, bone-deep, lusty attraction like what he felt right at this moment for Miss Charlene Singer.

The feeling had always been there but Mason had

never been able to act on it. He'd been running from his past and she'd been a vivid reminder of it. While he'd avoided her all those years ago because he'd been a kid and the fierceness of what he'd felt for someone so different from him had scared him, he'd avoided her every day since his parents' death because he couldn't avoid tying himself to a town he could no longer call home.

Until now.

Judging by Charlene's fast retreat, however, he'd be willing to bet that, for whatever reason, she wasn't nearly as anxious to act on that attraction. But he knew she felt it.

"...have to get together sometime," Lolly was saying.

Mason forced his gaze away from Charlene and back to the blonde whose mouth moved faster than an ornery calf trying to outrun a lasso.

"For old times' sake," she went on.

"I'm really busy getting settled in." Not that busy, he reminded himself. It had been a damned sight too long since he'd really cut loose. He'd spent the past eight months on a twenty thousand acre ranch in the Black Hills of Montana. Isolated. With only a marriage-minded kindergarten teacher to warm the sheets with.

Needless to say, he'd spent many a cold night because Mason had steered clear of any and all SOS women—smart, opinionated and sexy as all get out.

While he'd always liked his females sexy, he'd also liked them uncomplicated. Given the fact that he'd been on the road so much and hadn't been able to have a real relationship, he figured it was better to avoid the temptation entirely. No smart, opinionated, sexy woman was going to make him want to stay for more than one night.

That was all about to change.

"Do you remember that time on the fifty-yard line after the game with Waller High School?" Lolly asked him.

"I—" he started.

"Of course you do. Boy, we had such a good time. We could have a good time again." She tilted her head to the side and fluttered her eyelashes in a move that had seemed fresh and coy when they were kids. Now it seemed old and stale.

Because he was different now.

He wanted more than just a good time. He wanted a great time, and he wanted to have it with a woman who made him so hard and desperate that he couldn't see straight. Mason wanted what his parents had never had in their own marriage—the lust factor.

While Lolly was pretty, he didn't feel near the attraction he'd felt for Charlene Singer. Even so, he'd never been one to hurt a woman's feelings. While he'd set his mind on his future, there wasn't anything wrong with talking over old times.

"I could sure go for a burger over at the diner."

"I was thinking more dessert back at my place…" The rest of Lolly's words faded in the sudden commotion as the front double doors opened and Josh McGraw strode outside, a pretty redhead cradled in his arms.

"Excuse me a sec," Mason said to Lolly before striding up to his brother. "I'm assuming this is Holly." Mason smiled at the woman as Josh eased her to her feet.

"The one and only." Josh grinned, his blue eyes twinkling as he slid his arm protectively around her waist. "This is my younger brother, Mason."

"Younger by about five minutes," Mason reminded him.

"Five minutes and forty-five seconds," Josh corrected.

"It's good to finally meet you. My, but your eyes are green."

"We're fraternal triplets," Mason told her. "While we all look the spitting image of each other, our eye color is different. Josh got the baby blues and Rance, the youngest, has gold eyes."

"That's amazing." Holly spared Mason a smile before her attention shifted back to Josh. For the next few moments, they seemed to lose themselves in each other.

"Since you don't look madder than a wet hornet," Mason finally said, feeling suddenly awkward for one of the few times in his life, "I'm assuming she said yes."

"Damned if she didn't."

And damned if Josh didn't seem incredibly happy about the fact. The cynical gleam in his gaze had disappeared. His serious, intense expression had slipped away. His usual back-it-up-buddy air had faded.

He looked truly happy and content.

Mason felt a rush of envy. Despite all his professional success, his personal life wasn't anything to talk about. By necessity, he reminded himself. But now that he was taking over the Iron Horse the way he was always meant to, the way his mother had wanted, and continuing the family tradition, he could open himself up to a relationship with the right woman.

His gaze shifted in time to see the Lexus nose around the far end of the parking lot and pull onto Main Street. Charlie Singer was every bit the SOS girl he'd walked in on in the bathroom so long ago. Still smart and opinionated and sexy as all get out. Still staring at him with that open hunger in her gaze. Still stirring his interest and firing his fantasies.

But now, she was no longer off-limits.

"THE HAMBURGER IS definitely off-limits. Talk about your double whammy. Toxic red meat swimming in saturated fat."

Charlene glanced up from her menu at the man who sat opposite her in the booth at the Fat Cow Diner.

Dr. Stewart Connally had dark brown hair cut short and neat, and deep brown eyes. His jaw was freshly shaven, as usual, and his white button-up shirt was neatly starched and buttoned just one shy of his neck. A crisp white undershirt peeked from the small V and a gold Rolex glittered from his wrist. His lab coat rested on the back of the seat next to him. He wasn't a particularly attractive man with his slightly too large nose and a pair of eyes that sat a little too close together, but he made the most of what he had—namely a good physique—and he was neat.

It was their weekly lunch meeting and Charlene had been late thanks to Mason McGraw and the conversation about her underpants which had delayed her a good ten minutes.

As if her thoughts had conjured him, the bell on the door chimed and he walked in, Lolly Langtree on his arm.

He obviously didn't waste any time falling back into old habits, Charlene thought as she watched them slide into a nearby booth.

"...not having the hamburger, are you?" Stewart's voice pushed into her head and she shifted her attention back to the man who stared at her over his menu. Worry lit his brown eyes.

Charlene would have been touched by his concern, but she knew from previous lunch dates that he wasn't nearly as worried about her arteries as he was about having all that greasy temptation within arm's reach.

Stewart was six feet of fit, toned, tanned muscle with very little body fat. Less than nine point two percent, to be exact. A tidbit of information he shared on a regular basis with anyone and everyone who would listen.

She grinned. "I'm not in the mood for toxic red meat swimming in saturated fat."

"Good." Relief etched his handsome features as his gaze went back to the menu. "The fried catfish special is definitely a no-man's land, what with all the batter and oil and the steroids that Walt Jackson pumps into his fish before he stocks his pond." He studied the menu a few more seconds. "The egg salad's always a possibility provided they use a mayonnaise substitute."

"I feel like apple pie." While she didn't do chocolate, Charlene still indulged her sweet tooth. Not to mention, she needed something sweet after all that talk about chocolate and orgasms and…

Her gaze drifted back to Mason in time to see him glance up. His gaze locked with hers and her breath caught.

He wouldn't…

He did.

His eyes crinkled and his lips tilted at the corners and he actually *grinned* at her.

Her body—damn the superficial, traitorous thing—reacted accordingly. Her nipples pebbled and her insides grew tight and itchy and—

"Are you okay?" Stewart's voice broke the seductive spell that she'd been trapped in and yanked her back to reality.

"I—I beg your pardon?"

"You look flushed."

"It's really warm in here." She fidgeted against the vinyl seat. "Don't you think it's warm in here?"

"I'm rather comfortable myself."

She fanned herself with the edge of the menu and let loose a deep breath. "Maybe it's just me." Duh. "Maybe I'm coming down with something." A bad case of lust thanks to Mason and his grin.

"I could prescribe some antibiotics when I get back to the office."

"That's okay. I'm sure I'll be okay."

"I'll write the prescription anyway. In case you get sick with something while I'm away at that conference. There's a summer flu going around."

"Once I eat something, I'll probably feel a lot better." Charlene turned her attention to the waitress who approached.

"You don't know how lucky you are," Stewart told her after they'd placed their order—one apple pie à la mode and one grilled chicken salad with low-fat Italian dressing on the side. "Just catching a whiff of any type of dessert makes me pack on a few pounds."

Once upon a time, Stewart had been known at Romeo High as "Goodyear." As in the blimp. All that had changed when he'd gone away to college. He'd shed fifty pounds, packed on some muscle and had come home looking like he'd done a stint on *Survivor.*

"A protein-rich, low-fat diet and lots of exercise," he'd told Charlene. "Not to mention, pediatric residents barely have time to breathe much less eat."

But Skeeter McBee and his group of busybodies that sat near the doorway of the diner still swore they'd seen him eating Mongolian cockroaches during the last season.

"Are you sure you're okay?" Stewart reached across the table and took her hand in his. It was a friendly gesture that he'd made often during the course of their lifelong friendship.

One with little meaning behind it other than genuine like, since he'd yet to realize how perfect they were for each other.

Men were just so *slow* sometimes.

"I'm fine, really," she told him.

"You don't look fine. You look uncomfortable." As if he'd noticed the direction of her gaze, he turned and glanced behind them. "Lolly Langtree looks as trampy as ever, particularly with that low-cut dress and her new set of double D breasts. With the way she's fawning all over Mason McGraw, she might as well crawl into his lap." He turned back to Charlene. "I know people like that can make everyone else uncomfortable, but you can't let a snotty diva like Lolly bother you. Sure, she's got a heck of a body and a really great face and she shamelessly puts it out there for anyone and everyone, but it will all come back to haunt her one day." He shook his head in disgust.

"You mark my words, she'll fool around with the wrong married man and find herself staring down the barrel of a shotgun someday."

Because Stewart had endured so much name-calling as a kid, he'd yet to forgive and forget the people who'd made fun of him.

Namely Lolly and her diva friends.

"She's the last person you should let bother you," Stewart went on. "She isn't even in the same league as the two of us. We have self-respect. Class. Actual brains." He told her what she'd told herself time and time again all those years ago.

The trouble was, she didn't believe it now any more than she had back then.

"I'm a little tired, that's all."

"Good because we're having dinner with my parents on Friday before I leave Saturday morning and I would hate to have to cancel because you're sick. You know how Dad hates having his plans messed up." Judge and Mrs. Connally were perfectionists. Not a good thing for a boy who'd been very imperfect. But then he'd changed his appearance, graduated at the top of his class, and come home the perfect son—at least weight-wise. He'd been going out of his way to keep things that way ever since.

"Not to mention," he was saying, "it was hell to clear my schedule in the first place. Speaking of which—" he glanced at his watch "—I hope they hurry up. I've got a busy afternoon. I have several patients to see before I meet with Doctor Collier from Cherryville, who's agreed to fill in for me while I'm gone. We're having dinner at the Steak-n-Bake." The Steak-n-Bake was the nicest restaurant within a fifty mile radius of Romeo and the only place where they actually had linen napkins. It was located just off the main Interstate about twenty minutes outside of town and it had always been *the* date place on any given Saturday night.

Charlene had been there on occasion with her mother while growing up, but never with a date. Which spoke volumes for her social life. Or lack thereof.

"Are you packed yet?" she asked Stewart.

He smiled. "Done, and I used my new organizer suitcase. Fit everything into one bag with room to spare. You know, I'm really excited about this conference. I've got everything planned down to the minute." He smiled and seemed to lose himself in his thoughts before he noticed that Charlene was looking at him. He cleared his throat. "Um, that is, I just love learning new treatments. It's time consuming, but totally worthwhile."

"I've just started a new communication therapy with some of my patients, one I read about on the Internet," she added. "It's the latest thing and, so far, it seems to be actually working."

"Really? You'll have to fill me in on the details when I get back. And speaking of getting back…" He cleared his throat again as if to work up his courage.

"I, um, was thinking that when the conference is over and things settle down again, we really need to sit down and talk about us. We've been having lunch every week for how long now?"

"Two years."

"Two years is a really long time to see someone on a regular basis."

Plenty of time for Stewart to have realized that they were perfect for each other in a romantic sense. They were both professionals. They both enjoyed reading. They even had the same favorite color—beige. They were a match just waiting to happen.

"I'm getting back on Sunday morning, so maybe we can have an early dinner that night at the Steak-n-Bake. I think we need to talk about the nature of our relationship." Before he could elaborate, his beeper went off. "It's Bernice." Bernice was his nurse. "I hope Dr. Collier didn't cancel. I can't miss this trip." He gave Charlene's hand an affectionate squeeze and pulled his cell phone from his pocket to call his office.

Charlene closed her hand against the lingering warmth. A direct contrast to the overwhelming heat she'd felt when she'd handed Mason her business card and his fingers had brushed hers.

When Stewart touched her, she felt comfortable. Calm. Safe.

She never felt as if she was standing on the edge of a steep well, the shaft pitch-black, the bottom endless.

With Stewart, she could see what lay ahead. Their weekly lunch filled with talk about work and family. Their occasional Friday night dinner date—when he managed to carve time out of his schedule—always followed by talk about books or movies or world events. She could even envision the nice, satisfying sex they would have once he actually realized they were so compatible. If his beeper didn't go off, that is.

Nice.

The way it should be between good friends.

Her gaze shifted to Mason who'd just taken a gigantic piece of chocolate cake onto his fork. He slid the bite into his mouth and Charlene felt her own stomach tighten.

Mason wasn't the type of man to be friends with a woman. Nor was he a man to dim the lights, slide beneath the sheets and hold a woman tenderly in his arms the way she imagined Stewart would do.

Loud. Bright. Down and dirty.

She'd bet money that that's what sex with Mason McGraw would be like. If she'd been a betting woman.

But Charlene wasn't the type to gamble on uncertainty. She prepared for life. She contemplated it. She studied it with the various how-to books that lined her monstrous bookshelf. She planned it down to the last detail so that there were no surprises.

No excitement.

Charlene forced aside the last thought and turned her attention to the apple pie the waitress slid in front of her.

She didn't need excitement.

What she needed was a way to show the women of Romeo that it wasn't about the way they looked or dressed or what they cooked up in their kitchen that made them attractive to the opposite sex. A woman didn't have to turn herself into a flirtatious, outrageous diva like Lolly Langtree to attract a man. All she really had to do was be herself and let her personality shine through.

She needed to prove that to the women of Romeo. But even more, she needed to prove it to herself.

"Are you all right?" Stewart asked her again. "Because I've been talking and I don't think you've heard a word I've said."

Charlene forced a smile. "I really am tired." And rattled.

"Cancel your afternoon appointments and go home early," Stewart suggested. He smiled. "Doctor's orders."

She nodded.

Maybe after a good night's rest she wouldn't be thinking such ridiculous thoughts. Like how her coveted theory might be completely and totally off-base and her life's work useless.

Or worse, how she'd wasted so many years waiting for the perfect match to come along and give her the happily ever after she'd always dreamed about, only to find herself just this side of thirty and still very much alone.

Or how much she really needed a taste of Mason's chocolate cake.

And how much she really, *really* needed a taste of him.

3

"Dadblame it, Lurline! I told you to buy the high-fiber bran flakes."

The familiar male voice carried through the house to greet Mason when he opened the front door of the sprawling ranch house that sat in the heart of the Iron Horse.

He'd spent the better part of the day since he'd returned from town inspecting the north pasture. There were fences to be repaired, cattle to be rounded up and a host of other chores that had fallen by the wayside since his granddad had passed on a few months ago.

Josh had been seeing to things since the funeral while Mason finished up his last project as head of McGraw Ranch Management. But in the past few weeks, Josh had been preoccupied with Holly Farraday. Not to mention, Josh had never been much of a rancher at heart. As a teenager, he'd been more content under the hood of an old clunker than on the back of a horse. While he'd spent his free time back in high school learning how to fly a crop duster and had gone on to become a pilot and operate his own charter service out Arizona, he'd never lost his passion for cars. Now that he'd found *the* woman, he'd decided to sell his business, stay in Romeo and open up his own auto shop.

Mason was glad that his brother had finally made peace with his past—Josh had nursed a world of hurt over their father's infidelities—and so he wasn't the least bit angry that Josh had let things slide a little at the ranch.

"All bran flakes are high in fiber. That's what bran is," a female voice countered, pulling Mason from his thoughts. A voice that belonged to his great-aunt Lurline.

Lurline and her husband Eustess had moved in six years ago when Mason's grandfather had first been diagnosed with prostate cancer. Since all three grandsons were off making their own way in the world and they were the only living relatives within a spit and a throw, Lurline had said it was their duty to look after Romeo in his time of need.

He'd passed away eight months ago, but Mason and his brothers had insisted that the older couple stay on at the house. Lurline and Eustess were just a few birthdays shy of ninety. Lurline's memory wasn't what it used to be and Eustess suffered from severe arthritis. Their own kids had grown up and moved away, and they found themselves the ones in need of family now.

And Mason was in need of an extra strength Tylenol.

"There ain't a thing on this here box that says anything about these flakes being high in fiber. I want the ones in the light blue box that say it right there on the front."

"That's just fancy packaging to make folks think that they're getting something extra so they'll fork over a good fifty cents more for something that ain't worth more than two dollars in the first place."

Make that two Tylenol.

After an hour at the Fat Cow Diner, Mason had had a headache the size of the Grand Canyon. So big, in fact, that even an afternoon out in the pasture, with the sun beating down on him and the horse steady and strong beneath him, hadn't been able to ease the blasted throbbing. Lolly had wanted more than a walk down memory lane. She'd wanted a ride, so to speak, and Mason's refusal hadn't set too well with her. Not that she would be put off. That was one thing about Lolly and all the women like her. They were persistent.

The thing was, Mason didn't feel nearly as hot and bothered over Lolly as he was over a certain relationship therapist. And so all the persistence in the world wasn't going to change his mind.

Not this time.

Because at this point in his life, Mason McGraw wanted more than a roll in the hay.

He wanted forever.

"I want the cereal in the blue box," Eustess insisted while Mason contemplated opening the door and heading back out to the barn.

That's what he'd been doing for the past week. In between watching Josh mooning over Holly and listening to Eustess and Lurline arguing over everything, the only peace and quiet Mason had found was out in the pasture. Branding calves, rounding up strays or riding fence.

But Josh had declared his love and he was now at Holly's place working out the details of their future together. And probably working out, period.

Which meant it was just Eustess and Lurline standing between Mason and a good night's sleep.

He walked down the hallway toward the kitchen and the voices.

"Really, Eustess." His aunt Lurline was a tiny woman with curly white hair and glasses. She wore the same type of flower print dress she'd worn when Mason and his brothers had begged for chocolate chunk cookies and milk every Sunday after supper. This particular one was orange with black daisy shapes. "You're acting like a child."

"I'm actin' like a man who's wife refuses to do what she's told." Eustess was a foot taller than his wife, but thanks to his arthritis, he stooped so much that they almost seemed the same height. He wore overalls over a long-sleeved yellow shirt that buttoned up to his neck. His bald head glittered in the kitchen light.

"Nice night." Mason walked over to the stove and picked up a piece of his great-aunt's fried chicken.

"Good evening, dear," Lurline said, pausing to smile at Mason before she turned a murderous stare on her husband of sixty-something years. "First off, Eustess Luther Eugene Ketchum, you don't *tell* me a cotton pickin' thing." She wagged a finger at him. "You *ask*. And then, if I'm feeling my usual generous nature, I'll do it. If I'm not, you can darned tootin' go to the store and get your own overpriced cereal." Her attention shifted back to Mason and her smile returned. "There's gravy to go with that, dear."

"Mighty good gravy, too," Eustess added, clapping Mason on the shoulder before he eyeballed his wife. "That's the trouble with you. You're too damned tight with a penny, just like your mother."

"My mother was frugal. There's a big difference. And if you want to point fingers, you need to point one at your own mother. Why, that woman was the most bossy female I've ever met."

"Your mother was a gossiping busybody," Eustess countered.

"This chicken is out of this world," Mason said, eager to distract Lurline. But the dig at her mother had obviously pushed her over the edge.

"Well," she huffed, "your mother was a know-it-all. Too bad somebody drop-kicked the apple when it fell from the tree."

Eustess' gaze narrowed. "What's that supposed to mean?"

"That you ain't got the sense God gave a goose. Why, there are regular folks the world over who would give their right eye for that there box of bran cereal."

"No need. They're more than welcome to mine 'cause it ain't gonna do me a lick of good. I swear you're trying to kill me."

"If I was, believe you me, I would think of something a heck of a lot more painful."

"Ain't nothing more painful than stopped up plumbing. 'Cept maybe seeing you in that there orange dress."

"Why, you old geezer…"

"I think I'll just finish this upstairs," Mason said as he headed for the hallway. The arguing continued as if Mason hadn't said a word. The voices followed him clear across the house to the large bedroom he'd occupied as a kid.

He'd played high school football and he'd been good at it, but he hadn't loved it. Not like his baby brother, Rance, who'd gone on to play pro ball for the Dallas Cowboys until a knee injury had knocked his career out from under him.

Mason's passion had been rodeo.

Trophies for everything from calf-roping to bronc busting lined the walls. Dozens of buckles lined another shelf. His favorite lasso hung from one of the bedposts. His first saddle draped over the back of a chair.

It had been during his rodeo days right after high school that he'd realized the real ingredient to a lasting marriage.

Tucker Pierce had been the best bull rider on the circuit back then and a good ten years older than Mason. He'd been a country boy from the Texas Hill Country with a sharp Southern twang and a degree from the school of hard knocks. He'd been married to Linda, a Harvard-educated lawyer who'd come from old money. They'd been about as opposite as black and white, and yet they'd been the happiest couple he'd ever seen. Linda never missed a rodeo. Every Friday she would leave her fancy practice in Houston where they'd bought a house, and drive to whatever hole-in-the-wall town was hosting that week's ride. And after the rodeo, they would disappear into Tucker's RV and not come up for air until the next morning.

Mason had gone to the Pro Bull Riding Finals in Las Vegas a few years back and he'd run into them. They'd still been all smiles. Still happy. And going on twenty years of marriage.

Mason had once asked Tucker their secret and his friend had simply smiled and said, "It's called good, old-fashioned lust, buddy. We just can't keep our hands off each other."

Physical attraction.

That's what drew two people together. What kept them together. Mason's parents had had similar personalities and a shitload of things in common, but they hadn't had even the tiniest bit of physical attraction. And so their marriage had been a failure from the start. A farce.

It made sense, and it also made him that much more determined to do things differently in his own life.

Mason hung his hat on a peg near the door, sat down on the edge of the twin bed and pulled off his boots. While the room seemed smaller than he remembered, the house itself actually seemed bigger.

Then again, the last time he had been home had been for his grandfather's funeral.

There had been people everywhere then, filling up every nook and cranny. The same way they'd done when Mason's father had passed away after wrapping his GTO around an telephone pole. Mason had been thirteen and his father's death had come less than twenty-four hours after his mother had died in the hospital from an infection associated with a miscarriage.

His father had been running from his grief in that car, trying to outrun his pain.

But Mason had lived with his pain. He'd lived with the loneliness and the longing for a real home and a real family.

No more.

He was through dreaming about home. He was here now and he was staying. As for a real family... He intended to do something about that soon, starting with finding a woman. The woman. The one who turned him on and fired his blood, one who filled him with a lust so intense that he wouldn't be able to keep his hands off of her, just like Tucker had said.

"...I'd never married you in the first place. My momma warned me..." Lurline's voice carried through the open doorway.

Mason kicked the door closed and emptied his pockets out onto the dresser. His fingers paused on the crinkled business card and an idea struck.

He smiled.

While he, personally, didn't need any relationship therapy—he knew from seeing his parents' dysfunctional marriage that it took an intense physical attraction to make a relationship really work—he knew a couple who could definitely use Charlene's help. He was going to have a hell of a time getting any sleep with Eustess and Lurline at each other's throats.

They needed Charlene.

And Mason needed a good excuse to see her again because he had a hunch, and a hard-on, that told him she just might be the woman he was looking for.

"It's about time you showed up." Marge Winchell met Charlene at the door early the next morning.

Marge had been her father's secretary over at Romeo Savings & Loan since its grand opening in 1962, right up until he'd packed his bags, left his wife and job, to everyone's shock, and moved to Pennsylvania.

She'd stayed on at the savings & loan as secretary to the man who'd replaced her father, up until her favorite boss' daughter had graduated college and opened up her own practice. She'd been with Charlene ever since.

Marge's frosted hair was teased in the same beehive hairdo she'd sported at the bank's ribbon-cutting ceremony, a picture of which still sat on the corner of her desk. Bright pink lipstick matched the nail polish on her two-inch acrylic nails. Silver-framed cat's eye glasses perched low on her nose. She wore a white button-up blouse and a full pink skirt belted with a three inch black leather belt. Several pink plastic bracelets dangled from one bony wrist. She smelled of Aqua Net and Emeraude and the three Camels she allotted herself per day.

"Here's your coffee." Marge handed Charlene a steaming mug. "And your messages." The old woman shoved a stack into Charlene's other hand. "And the lecture notes that you wanted me to type up." The woman handed over a manilla folder which Charlene cradled in her arms. "And the chart for the nine o'clock patient."

"But we don't have a nine o'clock."

"We do now. The Patricks were waiting when I pulled into the parking lot. They said they needed to speak with you right away. They're in your office. Now, here's the morning mail, including a flyer for that seminar you wanted to register for last year, Getting in Touch With Your Inner Self." She set the colorful brochure on the growing stack. "The latest issue of *Psychology Today,* another advertisement for another seminar, Getting in Touch With Your Spouse's Inner Self, a few pieces of junk including coupons for the new bakery opening up over by the courthouse, the new *Science Digest,* a Frederick's of Hollywood catalogue."

"But I don't—"

"Wait a second." Marge snatched the catalogue back. "That's mine." She rifled through her stack. "Mine." She pulled out the Venus Swimwear Summer Sales Bonanza. "Mine." The latest issue of *Cosmo.* "And mine." She also took another catalogue for the new Xandria collection of sex toys. Then she made a face. "Definitely yours." She handed over the Abercrombie & Fitch. "You'd better hurry." She rounded Charlene and gave her a little push toward her office door. "The Patricks have been waiting for twenty minutes and it's been quiet the entire time."

"Really?" Charlene smiled. "The therapy must be working."

"That or they've bludgeoned each other to death." Marge deposited the leftovers on the corner of her desk. "I knew that coffee table book Stewart gave you for Christmas, *How to Can Your Own Vegetables,* would come in handy some day."

Charlene frowned. "It's signed by the author and

it was thoughtful. You know how much I love how-to books."

"*How to Ride 'Em Like a Rodeo Queen.* Now that's thoughtful, and darned useful. Forget decorating the coffee table. There's no man in his right mind who wouldn't want his woman to wear down the pages memorizing every cotton pickin' word of that."

Charlene eyeballed her secretary. "There's no such book."

"There sure enough is, and if Stewart had half a brain he would have bought it for you. Something's wrong with that boy, I'm telling you. No man in his right mind buys a woman a book about canning."

"He does if they're friends, which we are." For now.

"That's my point. No healthy, red-blooded American man, at least the ones I know, would be happy being friends with a woman unless he butters his bread on the wrong side. Are you sure he's not gay?"

"Yes." Sort of. She'd actually wondered the same thing for a while. But then she'd personally witnessed him salivate a time or two while watching a particularly attractive female contestant on *Jeopardy,* so she'd dismissed the notion. "He wants to talk about us when he gets back from his convention." There. Let Marge digest that tidbit of information.

"Is that so?"

"It most definitely is." Charlene smiled. "I think he's going to step things up and ask me to be his girlfriend."

"It's about time. Good friends." Marge snorted.

"Why, that's the silliest thing I've ever heard. You wouldn't catch me wasting my time with a man who just wanted to be my friend."

"He wants more. He just hasn't had time. He's a very busy man."

"Too busy to jump your bones? Sounds like he's afraid of commitment if you ask me."

She wanted to inform Marge that she wouldn't be contemplating a serious relationship with Stewart in the first place if he was the bone-jumping sort. She liked mutual respect and romance, with all of the lights out.

In her reality, that is.

She'd envisioned a few detailed bone-jumping scenarios in her fantasies, however. But Stewart had been nowhere around. Just a certain dark, delicious, hunky cowboy who smelled even better in person than she'd ever imagined.

Charlene forced her thoughts into taking a quick detour. "Stewart isn't afraid of commitment," she went on. "He's just careful about making major decisions."

"And too damned slow, if you ask me. Who needs a man like that?"

"I do. He's my soul mate."

Marge gave her an *are-you-serious?* look before she reached into the bottom drawer of her desk and retrieved a massive black leather purse. "Just tape the session and I'll transcribe it when I come back."

"Where are you going?"

"I've got a nail appointment. They couldn't see me at lunch on account of all the secretaries over at the courthouse scheduled during that time." She held up a hand and wiggled her fingers. "I'm trading in the gel and going acrylic this time."

"Sounds like a major life choice." Charlene turned back to the doorway.

"Don't get your Hanes in a wad. I'll be back before the next hour's appointment." Before Charlene could open her mouth, Marge rushed on. "It's Sheriff Miller. He's angsting about what to get the missus for their anniversary on account of he bought her a toaster last time and she pulled a gun and shot it clear to smithereens." As if Marge read the questions racing through Charlene's mind, she added, "She's going through The Change. Anyhow, he doesn't want to screw it up this time, so he thought you could help him out."

"I'm surprised he doesn't just order an Ultimate Milk Chocolate Orgasm from Sweet & Sinful and be done with it."

Okay, Charlene knew she sounded catty but it had been a stressful night. One spent tossing and turning, her thoughts alternating between Mason McGraw and Ultimate Orgasms and the possibility that maybe, just maybe, she was dead wrong when it came to relationships.

Sure, Stewart was coming around, but it had taken him long enough.

Because they lacked that intense physical attraction she'd felt for Mason McGraw?

Yes.

No.

She didn't know anymore.

"The sheriff actually mentioned Sweet & Sinful," Marge continued. "Said he'd thought of it, but his wife's on a diet and he doesn't want her to think he's insensitive."

"That's smart."

"That's what I told him. I also said to buy her some slinky panties, but he said he wanted to hear it from the expert."

Charlene smiled, juggled her armload of books and files and stepped inside her office. At least there was one person in town who still thought of her as the expert.

"Good afternoon," she said to the couple who sat on the small loveseat opposite a large, leather captain's chair.

Charlene set her burden on the desk before walking around and sinking down into the soft, brown leather opposite her longest-running clients.

The Patricks had come to her three years ago. After twenty-two years of marriage, they'd feared that they were drifting apart. They wanted to recapture the closeness they'd shared early in their relationship. The deep level of intimacy they'd felt when they'd witnessed the birth of each of their children, when they'd bought their first house and planted their first tomato garden.

They wanted to get to know each other again and stop their constant bickering.

Charlene had separated the two and administered in-depth personality tests which had determined that they were well-suited for each other and, therefore, ideal candidates for therapy.

They shared the same interests, the same core values and beliefs, and they both dotted their *i*'s with circles rather than dots. They both validated one another on every level. Talk about fuel for intimacy.

Charlene had prescribed one hour of conversation per day with a specific topic for each session. According to Charlene's notes, they'd just finished a month of "I like (blank) because…" The goal was to verbalize one's feelings, as well as to learn to see things through the other person's eyes. Day one had been flowers. Day two meatloaf, and so on until they'd hit the end of the month and the pièce de résistance "I like you because…"

Judging by the way that they sat on the sofa, thigh to thigh, hands clasped, fingers entwined, the "discovery" therapy had finally worked.

"So." Charlene smiled. "I see things are going well."

"They couldn't be better." Tina Patrick smiled at her husband. "Why, it's just like when we first met."

Tom Patrick winked. "Except I creak a lot more because of my arthritis and we don't have a curfew."

"And we use a sugar substitute because of my diabetes."

"I'm afraid I don't understand."

"For the Ultimate Orgasm. We did that last night, but we're going to try the Chocolate Fudge Body Bon Bons next time. I'm going to mix it up wearing nothing but my high heels and some red lipstick."

"I really love red," Tom said.

Ultimate Orgasm. The words echoed in Charlene's head as the truth settled in.

"But I thought you wanted to reconnect?"

"We reconnected plenty last night," Tom said.

"I meant an emotional reconnection."

"We haven't had sex in over a year," Tina said. "Trust me, it was emotional."

"What about talking?"

"We talked a little, too," Tina told her. "About how good the dessert tasted, and then about how good I looked and then about how we wanted to, you know, have sex."

"And then we stopped talking," Tom added.

"What about the conversation topics?"

"We've been doing them," Tina said. "And what we realized is that we're bored. That's why we've been drifting apart. There's only so much you can say about *Wheel of Fortune*. Hearing Tom go on about it just made me want to slit my wrists."

"And hearing Tina talk about her love of gerbera

daisies made me want to slip a noose around my neck and put myself out of my misery," Tom laughed.

"We needed to stop all the yapping and start having orgasms again," Tom continued.

"Lots of orgasms," Tina added.

What was it with all the orgasms lately?

"There's more to a relationship than just having a climax," Charlene told them. "It's about a meeting of the minds, as well as the bodies. It's about truly connecting. The fact that you two want to have more sex is good, but it's no reason to give up on the discovery therapy. Without effective communication, the sex is just gratuitous."

"Gratuitous sex is fine with me," Tom said.

"Me, too," Tina added.

"That's why we came by today, Doc." Tom glanced at his wife. "We wanted to tell you that we're going to take a break from therapy and go it on our own for a while."

"We're going to use the money for a new wardrobe," Tina added, her gaze hooked on her husband's. A smile touched her lips, as if they shared some great secret that Charlene wasn't privy to. "Tom really likes me in bustiers and fishnet stockings, and that stuff can be real expensive." She shifted her attention to Charlene. "You understand, don't you?"

"Um." Charlene licked her lips. "Of course," she managed to respond.

Not.

"Thanks, Doc," Tom said.

"That's right," Tina added. "We couldn't have done it without you."

"But you said the therapy didn't work."

"It didn't, but if I hadn't seen you at the lodge yesterday while I was across the street getting my hair done, I never would have stopped in for that luncheon. That hand-out about appealing to your partner's senses was a real eye-opener."

Not bunk. Or nonsense. Or propaganda.

"You saved our marriage," Tina declared as she got to her feet.

"You saved your own marriage." Charlene stood on trembling knees. "I'm just here to guide you through the process."

A process that now included high heels and bustiers, mouth-watering desserts and mindless, gratuitous sex. She tamped down on her rising nausea and tried for a smile.

"Take care and the best of luck to the both of you," she told the Patricks.

And then she did what any woman would do when her entire belief system had just been up-ended—she gathered her courage and faked it through the rest of the day's appointments.

On the way home, she stopped off at the nearest convenience store for a pint of Ben & Jerry's Cherry Garcia with a side of Chunky Monkey.

And then she sat in the parking lot with the engine of her Lexus running and ate her way to the bottom of both.

4

CHARLENE GATHERED up the empty ice cream containers and her briefcase, and climbed from her car. She tried to ignore the guilt that churned away inside her as she made her way up the front walk of the large two-story colonial that had once belonged to her parents.

Impossible.

She could practically feel the zits popping out all over her face. And all because of the Patricks and their announcement that her services—her basic values and beliefs—were no longer needed.

Okay, so it wasn't entirely their fault. They'd been the icing on the proverbial cake. It had all started with Holly Farraday and her aphrodisiac desserts.

Before Holly had come to town, Charlene had never considered physical attraction and sex as key components of a relationship. She'd just dismissed Stewart's failure to recognize her soul-mate potential with various excuses. He was too busy. He was too shy. He was too socially inept.

But with everyone jumping onto the orgasm bandwagon, she'd started to think that maybe, just maybe, he'd failed to take their relationship beyond friendship because he just didn't find her lustworthy.

It wasn't as if she had a hot body or a great face. She was average. But then, so was Stewart. That was part of the reason they were so perfect for each other.

His statement at lunch about wanting *to talk,* had given her hope that maybe she wasn't totally clueless. But then the Patricks had deflated that hope like a sharp knife to a balloon, and she was back to wondering if *she* wasn't the one full of bunk.

Figure in a rather embarrassing conversation with Mason McGraw, not to mention her awkward reaction to him—she'd rambled on about her underwear for heaven's sake—and she was definitely on a downward spiral.

Even more, she couldn't seem to stop thinking about him. Fantasizing.

Not such a big deal, considering the fact that she'd been doing that for most of her life. But since she'd seen him up close and personal, her fantasies had taken on new dimensions. She knew what he smelled like. She knew how warm he felt and how rough his fingertips were when they brushed hers.

Ugh.

The only bright spot in her entire day was seeing the package sitting on her doorstep when she reached the front porch.

She unlocked the front door and turned the doorknob. Inside, she flicked on the light, set her briefcase on the floor, hung her purse on the coat rack that sat next to the door and retrieved the package.

After tossing the ice cream containers into the kitchen trash, she made her way back to the living room and settled on the sofa. She smiled as she unwrapped the books she'd ordered on-line last week. *How to Make the Perfect Quiche* and *Building Your Own Barbecue Pit*. While she didn't actually have the time to do either activity—she spent her days preparing for her classes in the fall and working with her patients—she liked knowing that she was armed and ready should any free time present itself. She knew that one day her practice would slow and her lecture would lose its popularity. Then she would finally have the opportunity to try some of the interesting projects that filled the how-to books lining her bookshelf.

In the meantime, she could at least read about them.

Charlene took her new books and headed upstairs. She'd been the proud owner of the large house for over six years now, but thanks to her busy schedule, the place still looked the way it had when she'd been growing up. The only exception was the sizeable bookcase she'd bought for the living room to house her collection of how-to books. Otherwise, it was as if time had stood still.

Family portraits lined the winding staircase leading up to the second level. Her mother's prized chandelier—which she'd gotten at an estate sale for a steal—hung in its usual spot in the foyer. It was the only indulgent looking item in the otherwise low-key house.

The interior had been decorated years ago in neutral tones, the furniture a decent quality but simple. Functional. Her mother hadn't been concerned with impressing her father's bank colleagues or making a good showing down at the ladies' auxiliary so much as she'd been focused on holding tight to the family's money. She'd been obsessed with saving for the proverbial rainy day since she'd grown up in a steady downpour as the daughter of a poor farmer. While she'd married into a stable and comfortable life as the wife of a bank president, she'd never forgotten her roots.

She'd never stopped worrying, and so by the time Charlene's father had left, they'd accumulated a sizeable chunk of money that had been split right down the middle. Her father had taken his share and moved to Pennsylvania where his family had originally hailed from, and he now worked with a distant cousin as a financial consultant.

Her mother would still be eating bologna sandwiches for lunch every day and counting her pennies if not for a mild heart attack seven years ago. All the stress of scrimping and saving and raising a child on her own finally caught up with her. She'd realized then, after a triple bypass, that she couldn't use her nest egg if she was six feet under. She'd stopped hoarding and started living then. She'd signed over the house—which she'd been awarded in the divorce settlement—to Charlene and used her savings to purchase a top-of-the-line recreational vehicle. She and her widowed sister were now cruising through the South, namely Florida, and enjoying life.

At least, her mother said she was enjoying life. But in all the years since the divorce, Charlene had yet to see her really smile.

Likewise, she hadn't seen her father smile much either when she'd gone up to Pennsylvania or he'd come south for the occasional visit.

If she hadn't known better, she might have suspected that they actually missed each other. But she knew better. Her parents couldn't stand each other. They'd been in the same room only once since the divorce, at Charlene's high school graduation, and they'd made it a point to sit on opposite sides of the auditorium. They wouldn't even talk about each other.

While Charlene wasn't totally convinced that her mother enjoyed the whole RV thing, she kept her doubts to herself and wished her mother well. Personally, Charlene could never just up and leave everything, heart attack or not.

She liked waking up every morning in the same bed, in the same house, in the same town. She liked going to her office. She liked the drive to College Station three times a week for her lecture during the semester. She liked seeing the same faces day in and day out. Sure, she was a little tired of coming home to an empty house, but that problem would be resolved just as soon as Stewart came to his senses.

If he came to his senses.

The thought lingered in Charlene's mind as she set the books on her nightstand and peeled off her clothes. A few minutes later, she headed into the bathroom for her nightly facial scrub.

Leaning over the sink, she studied her reflection in the mirror.

No zits.

Yet.

But her fall from grace had only happened an hour ago. She had no doubt she would wake up with a face full. And so she not only scrubbed her face extra hard for the next five minutes, but she slathered on a heavy-duty zinc ointment afterward. It wasn't the most attractive way to sleep, but then she didn't actually have anyone to impress.

Not that she would have avoided the ointment just to impress her significant other. Stewart liked her for her, not what she looked like. Only a man like Mason McGraw would be turned off by a face covered with zinc. The superficial jerk.

She caught a glimpse of herself in the dresser mirror as she climbed into bed. Okay, so maybe she wouldn't blame him. She was a far cry from the daring divas he'd dated during high school. No wonder he'd never bothered to notice her. Yikes, from the look of her, she was surprised he hadn't run the other way.

Stewart, on the other hand, was just the opposite. He wasn't the least bit swayed by a woman's beauty or lack thereof. In fact, he hated women who primped and prettied just to catch a man's attention. He also hated the flirting and the flaunting. Bottom line, he hated the daring diva and everything she stood for.

He preferred a woman with inner beauty.

A woman with brains.

A woman who could appreciate a book entitled *How to Can Your Own Vegetables*.

"How To Ride 'Em Like a Rodeo Queen. Now there's a thoughtful gift."

Marge's words echoed in Charlene's head and she couldn't help herself. She headed downstairs to the small study where she kept her computer. A few minutes later, she clicked on her Internet Explorer and went to her favorite online bookstore. She typed in the outrageous title and hit Search, and nearly fell off her chair when the site found a match.

Marge had been right. There really was such a book. Before she could stop herself, she hit the Add To Cart button and went to Check-out. Not that she was interested in riding anyone like a rodeo queen. She just wanted to see the outrageous book for herself.

Now if there'd been a text on how to turn herself into a bonafide daring diva, or at least a convincing one, she would not only have purchased it, but had it shipped overnight.

If she could turn herself into the exact type of woman Stewart detested—on the outside—then maybe, just maybe, she could prove her theory.

Regardless of the way she looked, she would still be the same person inside. If he was still attracted to her, it would be because he saw beneath the surface to the real woman beneath. The personality.

If?

There was no *if* about it. It was all a matter of *when* and she could prove it.

Forget a how-to book. Charlene had been writing course synopses for her college students for years. With the right resources, she could formulate her own step-by-step plan to turn herself into a daring diva.

When Stewart returned from his conference and witnessed the new Charlene, he would still want her and, thereby, reaffirm her belief that it was a meeting of the minds that forged a solid, lasting relationship between two people.

She toyed with the idea as she shut off the lights and crawled into bed. She could make a convincing transformation on the outside if she put her mind to it. She could flaunt and flirt and wear her skirts up to there and her blouses down to here. She could.

But it wasn't the good doctor she flaunted and flirted with when she closed her eyes.

It was Mason McGraw.

And like he always did in her fantasies, he flirted back with her.

And told her how beautiful she was.

And how smart.

And how irresistible.

Fat chance as far as reality was concerned, but this was her fantasy where anything was possible.

Where even a hottie diva magnet like Mason could fall for a Plain Jane groupie like Charlene.

"HERE'S YOUR COFFEE." Marge met Charlene at the door early the next morning. But instead of handing her the mail, she tucked a strand of Charlene's hair behind her ear and swatted at some invisible fuzz on Charlene's pink blazer.

"What are you doing?"

"Making sure you're ready. Hurry up and drink." She motioned to the coffee cup. "You need all the pep you can get."

"What are you talking about?"

"There's a surprise waiting for you in your office." Marge smiled. "Think fantasy. Your hottest, wildest fantasy."

"The Patricks changed their mind?"

"Girl, you need to re-evaluate your priorities. I'm talking about a man." When Charlene started to open her mouth, Marge shook her head. "Stewart doesn't qualify. I'm still not convinced he's one hundred percent heterosexual."

"How about Walter Cronkite?"

Marge shook her head. "You're hopeless. Not a sexy bone in your body."

"I don't know about that." The deep, husky voice slid into Charlene's ears and she turned to see Mason standing in the doorway to her office.

"I... How long have you been standing there?"

"Long enough to know that you like Walter Cronkite and Stanley isn't exactly in the running for any machismo contests."

"His name is Stewart."

"Ha! The only contest he might win would be for giving the most boring Christmas gifts," Marge added, joining in. "He bought her a book. A boring, non-sexual book." Mason grinned and Charlene frowned.

"Don't you have work to do?" Charlene told Marge as she gripped her coffee mug and walked toward Mason. He stepped aside while she preceded him into the office.

Once she'd settled behind her desk, with several feet of wood and space between them, she drew a deep breath. "What brings you here?"

"I need some therapy." At her raised eyebrow, he added, "I, personally, don't need the therapy. It's my great-aunt and -uncle. They argue constantly and it's driving me crazy."

"Where are they?"

"I dropped them at the diner for breakfast. I

wanted a few minutes to talk to you before I brought them over."

"I see. So they don't realize there's even a problem."

"Oh, they know there's a problem, all right. I told them so this morning, right before I informed them that we were coming to talk to you. But they're each blaming the other."

"Blame aversion. That's normal. Neither wants to own up to the responsibility that they're harming their marriage." Charlene jotted down a few notes, eager to do something other than stare at Mason and think about how good he looked in his jeans and blue T-shirt, his dark hair still damp from a shower.

"So can you help?"

"Will they agree to cooperate with me?"

"Once I tell them that they cooperate or I'm sending them to live with their oldest daughter, Connie. She's been itching to check them into a retirement center for years."

"That sounds really manipulative."

"It's effective." He shrugged. "I wouldn't really do it, though. They were there for my grandfather when he needed them and I owe them for that. But they don't know that."

"I'm sorry about your grandfather."

He lowered his gaze. "He was in a lot of pain. He's at peace now."

"I'm sorry about your parents, too."

He glanced up. "That was a long time ago."

"I know. I just never had the chance to tell you back when we were kids."

He stared at her as if trying to figure her out. "Thanks," he finally said. "So can you help my aunt and uncle?" he asked again.

She nodded. "If they both agree to go along with the recommended therapy."

"How long do you think it will take?" Mason raked a hand through his hair. "I'm not getting any sleep."

"It depends. First I'll have to administer personality tests to determine if they're even compatible."

"They're obviously compatible. They've been married over sixty years."

"I realize that, but some people spend their entire lives with the wrong person. Despite the length of their marriage, they might not fit together."

He eyed her, a knowing glint in his gaze. "Sugar, they've got eight kids. I'd say they fit."

The word *sugar* echoed in her head and sent a rush of heat to every major erogenous zone.

Charlene stiffened and tried to tamp down her fierce response. "That's physically," she told him. "I'm talking about an emotional fit. That's much more important than sex. There are couples the world over who are happy together and they never have sex. What they have is a deeper connection."

"I'd like to see you prove that."

Me, too.

The thought rooted in her head and an idea struck.

A stupid, far-out, ridiculous idea that she quickly dismissed.

But then Mason grinned at her and her thought process short-circuited and damned if the crazy idea didn't find its way back in. And this time it seemed positively brilliant.

She stared at Mason with his sexy grin and bedroom eyes and his history of pretty, empty-headed conquests. If anyone was an expert on the subject of daring divas, it was Mason. If anyone could turn her into that exact type of woman, the kind Stewart totally despised, it was Mason.

If anyone could help her prove her theory to the women in town and, most of all, to herself, it was Mason.

Her hands trembled at the prospect and she licked her suddenly dry lips. Her nerves went on high alert and a warning blared in her head.

Are you crazy? This is your fantasy man, of all people. You can't just come out and proposition him.

Then again, it wasn't as if she was going to act on the lust raging inside of her and ask him for sex.

She only wanted his advice.

Yeah? And I've got some beachfront property smack dab in the middle of Kansas that you might be interested in.

"So how much is this going to cost me?" he asked her.

Charlene shushed her raging hormones and focused on the practicality of the matter. She needed him. He needed her. Completely nonsexually, of course.

Of course.

She smiled. "What do you say we take it out in trade?"

5

"IT'S A LOT BIGGER than I thought it would be."

Charlene's surprised voice echoed in Mason's head as he killed the truck engine and stared through the windshield at the legendary building that sat just off the highway headed toward Austin.

About a hundred years ago, the place had been nothing more than a two-story tin barn. Fifty years ago, its owner, a farmer by the name of Herman West, had spruced it up with a coat of red paint, installed a jukebox and opened up shop serving homemade moonshine. His daughters—all ten of them—had done the serving and Wild West had been born.

Wild West was no longer a family affair. The girls had aged and others had been hired to take their place and the jukebox had been replaced with a live disc jockey. But Herman was still the driving force. Still standing behind the bar every night and serving up his famous moonshine—his whiskey recipe had been patented and was now bottled and distributed in all fifty states.

"I should have expected it to be this big," Charlene's soft voice slid past his thoughts again and made his heart do a double thump. "It *is* rumored to be the largest men's club in Texas."

"I don't know if that still holds true." Mason eyed the legendary motto painted in giant white letters on the side of the building. *Beer, Babes and Barbecue!* "But it's definitely the oldest."

And the most notorious, which was why he'd driven Charlene out here for their first consultation regarding her diva transformation.

A daring diva? She didn't need to transform herself in order to prove that similar personalities were the foundation needed for a solid, lasting relationship. She would never be able to prove such a thing because it wasn't true. Besides, she didn't need to transform herself. He liked her just fine the way she was, and so he'd brought her here to scare some sense into her. Maybe she'd change her mind about her ridiculous plan.

"I've come up with a basic plan that includes three distinct areas I'll need to work on," she'd told him right after she'd propositioned him—free therapy for his aunt and uncle in return for his expert opinion on all things diva.

"First, I need to look like a daring diva. Then I need to move like one. Then I need to learn to act like one. I'll do the research, pick out the clothes and various hairstyles and such, and all you have to do is give me your expert opinion. We can meet at the

diner for lunch every day for a consultation. Then, by the end of two weeks, we should have made it through all three points. What do you say?"

He should have said no. Instead, he'd pictured her sitting across the lunch table from any number of single, available men in town who would jump at the chance to offer their expert *opinion* to a beautiful, sexy woman like Charlene, and he'd heard himself say yes.

"There are an awful lot of people here," she continued, her soft voice drawing him back to the present. It was only Thursday night, but the parking lot was already overflowing with cars and pickup trucks. "I bet it draws a lot of tourists."

"Some, but it's the locals that keep the place in business."

His gaze shifted to the entrance in time to see a handful of men approach. They were typical customers—all decked out in their starched Wranglers and button-down western shirts, their hair slicked back, their boots polished. Most wore cowboy hats with the exception of one who sported a Texas Rangers ball cap. The double doors swung wide and a popular country song blasted out into the parking lot, along with a cloud of smoke that quickly swallowed the group.

Mason glimpsed the blonde working the doorway. She wore the same Wild West uniform—an itty bitty leather vest, matching bikini bottom and leather chaps—that he remembered from his last visit several years ago. A friend he'd graduated high school with had gotten married and Mason had been in charge of the bachelor party. Because there was no better place than Wild West to get loud and rowdy and out-of-control while watching the prettiest girls this side of the Rio Grande.

Hell, they went beyond pretty. They were hot, with long legs and big breasts and plenty of curves in between just the way he liked. The kind of women who sent a man's common sense running for the hills and made his dick stand up and holler *yee-hahhh!*

His gaze slid to Charlene who stared through the windshield as if she was watching a movie at the drive-in. With her conservative gray slacks and white button-up blouse, she spelled *tame* with a capital T. She wore her silver-blond hair pulled back into a simple ponytail, her face void of any makeup except a flesh-colored lipstick that plumped her bottom lip and made him want to suck it into his mouth and nibble.

Bye-bye, common sense.

Yep, he needed to turn her off this whole cockamamie notion. She looked good the way she was. Too good if his stiff cock was any indication. The last thing she needed was to walk around flaunting herself.

He wasn't going to let her do it, and so he'd brought her here.

"If you really want to flaunt your stuff, you need

to see how the pros do it," he'd told her when he'd shown up at her house to go over the details of their arrangement.

Before she tackled the neatly-typed, three-point plan for her transformation—the looks, the moves and the attitude—she needed to do a little careful observation.

What Mason really intended to show her was that she was about to bite off more than she could chew. She was too sweet, too classy, too wholesome to be a wanton woman. Not to mention, her whole theory about an emotional connection being the key to a lasting relationship was nothing but bunk. The only thing Charlene stood to learn with this whole transformation nonsense was how to use a can of Mace on the horny guys who'd come crawling out of the woodwork once they got a glimpse of the new Charlene.

It was time to give her a healthy dose of reality.

As if on cue, the doors swung wide again and two men barreled out into the parking lot, their arms locked around each other as they fought to get the upper hand. A small group followed them, hooting and hollering for their favorite, along with an attractive redhead wearing a face full of makeup and the minimal Wild West uniform. Her ample cleavage pushed and strained against the tiny vest as she waved her arms and shouted for the men to stop.

"Are those two men fighting?"

"They're not two-stepping, darlin'." Mason made

a big show of threading his fingers together and cracking his knuckles. "How's your right hook?"

"My what?"

"Not that you'll have to use it. But things can get sort of rough in there and I'd feel better if I knew you could hold your own."

"I'm sure I can. I mean, it's been a while, but the last time I used it, it worked pretty good."

His gaze swiveled to her. "You actually hit someone?"

She nodded. "My cousin Ronnie. We were teenagers and he was forever calling me names when our folks would get together for Sunday dinner. Then one Sunday, I'd had enough. He opened his mouth and I let him have it."

"You actually hit someone."

"I gave him a bloody nose and knocked out a tooth. He never called me another name." Charlene's gaze shifted back to the men grappling near the entrance. Excitement lit her gaze. "I've never actually seen a real fight before. I mean, there was me and Ronnie, but it wasn't much of a fight. One punch and he went down for the count." Her hands went to the door handle. "Let's get closer."

Closer? Wait a minute. Wait a cotton-pickin' minute.

This was the part where she was supposed to realize that being in a place like this could be dangerous. She was supposed to change her mind. Then she would demand that he take her home where a sweet, classy good girl like her belonged.

Charlene was halfway to the entrance when he finally caught up to her.

"Wait a second." He grabbed her by the shoulder and spun her around. "I don't think this is such a good idea."

"It's great."

"It's stupid. You don't belong here."

"That's the whole point. I need to see how the other half really lives—how they walk and talk and dress—if I want to join them."

"You'll attract all kinds of jerks."

"Really?"

"Don't look so happy about the prospect."

"But I am. That's the whole purpose of this. If I'm attracting men, then I'm right on target with the transformation. Wild, wanton women attract men. It's what they do."

"It's also a damned sight dangerous. You could find yourself in a compromising position."

"Like what? Having two men fight over me?" *In my dreams,* her gaze seemed to say. That same insecure gaze he'd glimpsed when she'd been rambling about her underpants in the parking lot. As if she'd never believe any man could be that attracted to her.

Mason barely resisted the sudden urge to pull her into his arms and prove her wrong.

"I'm a grown woman with a Ph.D. in psychology," she told him. "I can handle myself."

"Is that so?"

"Of course."

"Then let's see how you handle this." And he kissed her.

Mason was trying to scare her because he thought her plan was ridiculous.

Charlene knew that. She also knew that on a rational level it was a bit far-fetched, but it would work. She knew it. She felt it.

While he hadn't refused her offer, the startled look on his face when she'd proposed her three-point plan had made it perfectly clear that he thought she stood about as much chance of morphing into a daring diva as he did of becoming a monk.

And so the offer to take her on a field trip in the name of research had merely been a ploy to get her to the most notorious strip club this side of the Rio Grande and dissuade her from the transformation. He obviously thought if he surrounded her with a roomful of real hotties, she would realize she wasn't outrageous enough to be one of them.

He still saw her as the girl who'd gotten caught with underpants around her ankles. The girl who'd run out of that bathroom and fled the party as fast as her cheap designer knock-off tennis shoes had been able to carry her.

But she wasn't that girl. She'd grown up. She wasn't as easily embarrassed or discouraged. And she certainly wasn't scared.

Not at this particularly moment, anyhow.

There wasn't anything frightening about the way Mason's lips covered hers, his tongue pushing deep to tangle with hers. For several frantic heartbeats, she couldn't think or breathe, much less react. She just stood there, her heart pounding in her ears, shock gripping her senses as his mouth ate at hers.

And then he growled low and deep, as if he hadn't had anything quite so good in a long, long time.

The sound struck a chord inside of her and her mouth opened.

His arms slid around her and he pulled her flush against his hard length. She pressed even closer, sliding her hands up his chest and curling her fingers around his neck. His skin was rough and warm beneath her palms and heat vibrated through her, pausing at several major erogenous zones along the way—her nipples and her belly button, the insides of her thighs and the backs of her knees—until her entire body burned. He tasted every bit as good as she'd imagined he would all those years ago. As good as all the rumors claimed.

Better, in fact, because this wasn't hearsay or some teenage fantasy. He was real, right here, right now, and he was really kissing her.

Mason McGraw was *kissing her.*

The thought sent a surge of satisfaction through her, followed by a rush of disbelief.

Mason McGraw was kissing *her?*

Just as the question rushed through her mind, the kiss ended and he pulled away.

Disbelief lit his gaze before his expression closed, as if he couldn't quite believe what he'd done. As if he regretted it.

She didn't blame him. All she'd done was kiss him back and already she wished she hadn't.

It was one thing to think about kissing him and quite another to actually do it. To feel his lips on hers. To want to feel them again even though she knew the kiss had been nothing more than a way to emphasize the truth—she didn't belong here. Not at a strip club, and certainly not in his arms.

Not yet.

"I told you I can handle myself."

"That wasn't handling. That was giving in. *Participating.* Christ, Charlie, if a guy comes on to you, you're supposed to knee him in the groin or ask for help. You're not supposed to kiss him back."

She shrugged and tried to ignore the way her nerves buzzed when he said her nickname. "What if I want to kiss him more than I want to knee him?"

"Do you?" If she hadn't known better, she would have sworn there was a trace of desperation in the question.

But, of course, she knew better. Men like Mason

McGraw weren't attracted to women like Charlene Singer. It was just wishful thinking on her part. A fantasy come to life. Now if she'd been wearing a teeny, tiny leather vest and some chaps…

She turned just as a giant-sized cowboy pushed between the two men and broke up the fight.

"You all settle down, come on back inside and have a drink. Either that, or get on home. We ain't toleratin' any of that here."

"He was lookin' at my gal." One of the men pointed around the cowboy to the other man who'd staggered back a few steps, his shoulders hunched as he fought for air.

"She ain't yore gal," the man managed to say, after he'd sucked down some oxygen. "She's mine. We're going out."

"You ain't going out with her 'cause I'm going out with her."

"Are you saying my gal is a two-timer?"

"I'm saying she ain't yore gal. She's my gal."

"Is not."

"Is too."

The men rushed at each other, sandwiching the bouncer as the fight broke out all over again.

"I mean it," the bouncer shouted above the commotion. "Y'all either get on back inside and get yourselves a drink, or get on home!"

"That's the best idea I've heard all night," Mason's voice came from behind her.

She nodded, her heart still pounding from the kiss, her lips tingling, as if it had been a real kiss and not a ploy to sway her from her plan. "I don't usually drink, but it does sound good."

"I was talking about the second suggestion." Before she could protest, he took her hand and tugged her around. Determination carved his handsome expression as he hauled her back toward his pickup. "We're going home."

HE'D KISSED HER.

Of all the lame-ass things…

Mason gripped the steering wheel and did his best to ignore the woman who sat next to him, her expression mutinous. He couldn't blame her. He'd hauled her all the way out there, only to act like a crazy man and drag her back home. She had a right to be mad.

At the same time, if she would have just realized how silly the whole thing was, the way she was supposed to, he wouldn't have had to pull a Dr. Jekyll on her. And he sure as hell wouldn't have had to kiss her.

The kicker was, he'd wanted to kiss her.

Hell, he still did.

But he knew she wouldn't likely welcome the advance again. He'd caught her off guard the first time, but Charlene Singer had made no secret that she didn't believe in lust and she surely wasn't going to gamble her future on it.

Mason tried to concentrate on the road instead of the thoughts rushing through his brain. Like how good she'd tasted and how sweet she smelled and how delicious she would look naked and draped across his hood, her nipples hard and ripe, her legs open and welcoming and...

"Damn, this truck is slow," he muttered as he pressed on the accelerator.

"Slow? You're driving like a bat out of hell."

"Are you saying you don't like my driving?"

"I'm saying you could slow down a little."

"I suppose you could do better."

"I don't know about better, but I could do it slower."

He'd meant to piss her off and stir a little animosity between them. But then she said *do it,* and the *it* sparked his imagination even more. Forget the hood. She was kneeling on a blanket near McGraw Creek, the moonlight playing off her gorgeous ass as he came up behind her...

He took a sharp left into her driveway and brought them to a jarring stop in front of her house.

"We're here," he announced.

Finally.

Thankfully.

Now all she had to do was open the door and slide out.

"Look, if you don't want to help me..." she said. He gripped the door handle and climbed out before she could finish. He walked around, opened her door and motioned her out.

"You don't have to help me," she announced, once she'd climbed out. "I just thought you were the obvious choice. I didn't mean to put you out."

Fine.

Thanks.

Have a nice life.

The responses echoed through his head and stalled just shy of his tongue when he glimpsed the sadness in her expression. The doubt.

"Look, I'm sorry about tonight."

"Don't be. I know you were just trying to make a point. A valid point. I'm nothing like those women at Wild West. I'm not half as pretty or as vivacious."

"You're right about that. You aren't half as pretty or as vivacious."

"Thanks a lot."

"You're more," he said before he could stop himself. Before she could voice the disbelief in her expression, he rushed on. "I just want you to be careful. Prepared. Understand?"

She nodded, but he could tell by the mix of emotions on her face that she hadn't a clue as to her effect on him.

"Tomorrow," he heard himself say. "I'll meet you for lunch."

"Could we make it Miss Jolie's? I really want to pick out some clothes."

"Miss Jolie's it is."

Relief flashed in her gaze before she gave him a stern look. "You better not be planning any funny business though, because I'm not changing my mind. I know this is a stretch, but I'm doing it. I have to do it. With or without your help."

That's what he was afraid of. "Don't get your feathers all ruffled." He winked. "I'll behave myself."

"I hope so."

So did he.

6

YOU'RE MORE.

The deep, husky murmur echoed in her ears and followed her up the front walk into her modest home.

Not that he'd actually said the words. She hadn't even seen his lips move. It had to have been wishful thinking on her part. Because no way would Mason McGraw think such a thing about Charlie Horse Singer.

He-llo? You're all grown-up now.

Even so, she was still as far removed from his type as a woman could get.

For now.

The hair on the back of her neck prickled and she knew he was watching her as she unlocked the front door and slipped inside. Once the door had been closed behind her, she scooted to the side and peeked past the drapes. She stayed there as he climbed into the truck, revved the engine and backed out of her driveway.

Charlene let the drapes fall back into place and headed upstairs. The upstairs hallway was lit, but otherwise, the house was dark. Quiet. Empty. A knot formed in her chest as she topped the stairs.

She hated coming home to an empty house, but that situation would soon be resolved once Stewart made a real commitment—

Her thoughts careened to a halt as reality hit her. Stewart. As in her soon-to-be *boyfriend.* As in, she'd just kissed another man while unofficially committed to someone else.

Unofficial being the key word. Stewart hadn't actually pledged his undying devotion to her, much less suggested that they see each other exclusively. Even so, it was just a matter of time before he asked her to take that next step. Two weeks to be exact, once he returned from the conference.

Meanwhile, she'd kissed another man.

Worse, she'd liked kissing another man.

Her mouth tingled and she licked her bottom lip. Of course she'd liked it. She'd kissed Mason McGraw. Her fantasy for as many years as she could remember. She would have had to have been dead not to have enjoyed it.

That didn't mean that she liked him. He was too full of himself for one thing. And too good looking, like one of those guys in *GQ*. The ones you knew had to be the product of skillful airbrushing because it simply wasn't possible for any man to have such intense green eyes and such a broad, masculine face and such a hot, hard body. And he grinned way too much. And—and this was the biggee—she had absolutely nothing in common with him.

No, she didn't like him. But that didn't change the fact that she'd kissed him back and enjoyed it. Even if Stewart was her soul mate.

At least she'd recognized as much. Meanwhile, Stewart seemed clueless, and so they weren't yet a real, committed, lay-around-the-house-and-scarf-down-ice-cream-and-watch-videos-every-Friday-night couple. With his hectic schedule, they barely saw each other. They'd yet to even hold hands in public. Sure, she'd met his parents, but that was it. He'd introduced her as his colleague. No "This is my girlfriend or my main squeeze or the woman I want to bear my children." He hadn't even hinted at a future together.

Even so, she intended to tell him about the kiss and how it didn't mean anything other than the fulfillment of a silly adolescent fantasy. He would understand because he'd had his own fantasies way back when. Of course, most of them had involved their high school physics teacher, Miss Worthenthorpe, instead of a real, accessible woman, but he'd had them nonetheless. She had no doubt that if Miss Worthenthorpe with her wire-rimmed glasses and MIT intellect walked up and planted one on him today, he would kiss her back.

Charlene sank down on the bed and dialed Stewart's cell number. He picked up on the fourth ring.

"How's it going?"

"Fine. Listen, I need to tell you—"

"Great, great," he cut in. "Listen, this really isn't a good time. I'm in the middle of dinner with Dr. Frankie Landau who did the study on herbal methods for treating pediatric colds." His voice grew muffled as if he'd put his hand over the mouthpiece. A softer, more high-pitched voice said something incoherent in the background. "Can you believe I'm sitting across from one of the leading pediatricians in the country?" he finally asked, his voice loud and clear once again.

"That's incredible." She tried to tamp down the strange sensation that something was wrong.

Something was wrong. She'd kissed Mason McGraw, of all people.

"I've really got to go," Stewart continued. "I'm really busy. I don't know if I can call you back."

"But I—" A click on the other end cut her off and she found herself listening to a dial tone.

So much for telling him tonight.

She would just fill him on everything if he did, indeed, take their relationship to the next level

If? What was it with all the stupid *if*s? *When,* she reminded herself. *When.*

She ignored the strange sense of relief that washed through her. She wasn't relieved. She was frustrated. She wanted to get the incident off her conscience and out of her head.

At the same time, a small part of her wanted to keep the information inside, to play it over and over in her mind a few times and milk as much satisfaction from it as she could. It was her fantasy come true, after all.

Or, at least part of it.

The other part she buried in the *Not in this lifetime* file, along with becoming a rock star, winning the lottery and marrying Brad Pitt.

A kiss was one thing.

Sex...well, that was completely out of the question. She was Charlie Horse Singer, after all, and he was Mason McGraw. They were worlds apart and the kiss had been nothing more than a tool for him to prove how totally clueless she was when it came to being wanton.

A daring diva wouldn't have stood there dumbfounded while the hottest man in town kissed her. Sure, she'd responded, but it had taken a while. Even then, she wasn't sure if her response had been good enough. Mason had oodles of experience. She couldn't begin to measure up to all of the other women he'd kissed.

You're more.

No way had he actually said those words. It had been her imagination. Her fantasies seeping into reality.

Even so, the notion sent a strange sense of satisfaction through her, along with a rush of restlessness. Her nerves tingled and as much as she knew she should peel off her clothes and crawl into bed—she had an early patient tomorrow—she couldn't seem to make herself. She was tired. At the same time, she wasn't sleepy. She was…exhilarated.

Thanks to Mason McGraw.

Forcing the notion away, she punched the button on her clock radio and a Gretchen Wilson song rushed from the speaker. She slid off her shoes and pushed to her feet. A few seconds later, she stood in front of her dresser and worked at the clasp of one earring. Her heart drummed and her lips tingled and her hands actually trembled.

She had to get a grip. She needed to stay focused on her three-point plan and prove her theory to everyone in town. That's all that mattered. Not Mason's kiss and its effect on her.

Then again, the kiss was important because it had showed her just how far she had to go to make the transformation. Determination could only carry her a certain distance. It wasn't about pretending to be a wild woman. It was about *becoming* that woman. The sort that wouldn't get all freaked out if Mason happened to kiss her. A woman bold enough and brave enough to initiate the kiss herself.

She finished with her earrings and set them in her jewelry box before unfastening her watch and placing it inside, as well.

Not that she wanted another kiss, mind you. Not from Mason McGraw.

She retrieved her favorite T-shirt—an oversized white cotton number that sported a picture of Minnie Mouse—from the drawer and turned toward her bed.

She'd satisfied the curiosity that had bubbled inside her all through high school. She knew now that Mason was every bit the incredible kisser she'd always thought he'd be and so she could lay that question to rest and turn her mind to other things.

Like what clothing colors drew a man's eye. And what hairstyles gave her that mussed, I've-just-rolled-out-of-bed-after-having-wild-sex look. And what Mason's kiss would feel like on other parts of her body.

The last thought rooted in her head as the fast country song ended and a sweet, hip-swinging Gary Allen tune poured from the radio. The same song she'd heard playing at Wild West when the doors had opened and she'd caught her first and last glimpse into the notorious strip club.

Before she could stop herself, she set the T-shirt aside, turned the volume up and closed her eyes. The music surrounded her and she caught herself swaying from side to side. She'd never been much of a dancer except in the privacy of her own bedroom.

In fact, she'd never actually danced with a man in public, with the exception of her father at the occasional wedding or anniversary party. He'd always loved Bob Wills and so she'd learned how to waltz at an early age. She had a hunch, however, that the girls at Wild West hadn't been waltzing to this. The music was too mesmerizing. The beat thrummed through her and made her want to roll her hips this way and that way and…

The thought faded as her eyes opened and she caught sight of herself swaying to and fro in the free-standing mirror that sat in the corner of the room. With her conservative trousers, her cover-everything-up blouse and her hair pulled back, she was a far cry from the scantily clad redhead at Wild West.

Before she could stop herself, she pulled the clasp free and let her blond strands tumble down around her face. With trembling hands, she slid the first button of her blouse free, then the next and the next. Her slacks followed until she wore nothing but her bra and panties.

She wasn't sure if it was the song echoing in her head and lulling her usually critical mind or if she was so tired that she'd passed the point of caring. Either way, her legs didn't look quite as gawky as they usually did, or her breasts quite as small.

Her white bikini panties rode low on her hips, making them appear more rounded, her limbs more proportioned. The lace cups of her Super Duty Wonderbra lifted her breasts and hugged them tight, plumping the flesh that spilled over the top. Her mouth seemed fuller, her eyes brighter, her cheeks pinker.

Prettier.

Even her moves didn't come across as all that amateurish. She undulated her hips in a slow, seductive rhythm and arched her breasts, and for the next few moments she wasn't in the safety of her bedroom. She was standing on top of a table, the neon lights blazing around her, a certain gaze pinned on her.

Watching.

Wanting.

She reached for the clasp of her bra. The cups fell apart and freed her breasts. They bobbed and bounced, the nipples rosy pink and ripe. She touched herself then, swirling her fingers around the dark areolas, until the tips throbbed for more. She trailed her fingers down her belly and traced the edge of her panties.

She wondered if the girls at Wild West touched themselves like this when they were on stage.

Maybe.

Probably.

She wondered if it felt half as good for them as it did for her now.

Good, but not great.

Not yet.

She hooked her fingers beneath the lacey straps of her panties and inched them down her legs until she stepped free and toed them to the side. Naked, she kept moving, teasing her body with her hands. She fingered her nipples and traced the slick flesh between her legs, all the while envisioning the reaction it would have on Mason.

The bob of an Adam's apple as he stared at her. The flash of hunger in his green gaze because he wanted her. The feel of his lips as he leaned forward and pressed them between her legs—

The thought stalled as the music ended and a commercial for Don's Pick Your Own Auto Parts blared over the speaker.

Charlene came to a dead stop. She stood there as Don talked ninety-to-nothing and studied her reflection.

The wild disarray of blond hair spilling down around her shoulders and framing her face. The faint indentation of her collarbone. The slope of her breasts. Her hard, wine-colored nipples. The shadow of her belly button. The slim V of gold pubic hair that covered her fleshy mound and disappeared between her long legs.

For the first time ever, she didn't feel the overwhelming urge to turn away or cover herself up. Sure, she wasn't all *that*, but she wasn't half bad either.

You're more.

The deep murmur echoed through her head again and she smiled.

Maybe there was some truth to it, after all.

MASON DIDN'T normally go around kissing women he had no intention of having sex with. But while his head knew Charlene Singer was completely off-limits, his damned cock hadn't quite got the message.

His groin throbbed and he shifted on the leather seat as he drove down Farm Road 25 toward the Iron Horse. He had his flaws—from his tendency to throw himself into his work and forget everything but the land and horses, to a weakness for Snickers bars and Eskimo Pies—but he wasn't a liar. He could tell himself that he meant to teach her a lesson, but deep down he'd been more interested in seeing if she tasted half as good as he'd anticipated.

She'd tasted better.

He licked his lips. Yep, she'd tasted better, all right. What's more, she'd responded with an intensity that had caught him off guard. No wonder he'd blurted out the truth to her.

You're more.

She couldn't be *more*. She had her mind set on another man, for Chrissake! On top of that, she didn't believe in any way, shape or form what he knew to be the gospel—that it was lust that mattered in a relationship. That it was the only thing that really mattered.

Which meant that if he pursued her, he would more than likely find himself smack-dab in the middle of another fling rather than a real relationship.

Like hell.

He'd been there and done that and he was sick of temporary relationships. The past sixteen years of his life had been about nothing but temporary.

No more.

He wanted something permanent in his life.

Something real. He wanted to succeed where his father had failed.

"A guy can't even go alligator wrestling anymore without all hell breaking loose." The deep, familiar voice sounded just to Mason's left as he stepped up onto the back porch and reached for the doorknob.

Light pushed through the kitchen window and cracked open the blackness to illuminate the man sprawled in a nearby cedar chair, his feet propped on a matching table.

With his dark hair and easy smile, Rance McGraw was the spitting image of his two brothers. Or he would have been if he'd had the good sense to get a sensible haircut, wear a decent shirt and a pair of starched Wranglers, and buy himself a cowboy hat that wasn't all bent out of shape.

But Rance had his own style.

He wore his hair down to his shoulders and lived in loud Hawaiian print shirts, raggedy board shorts and flip-flops. The only indication of his Texas roots was the beat-up straw Resistol that he'd been wearing since his sixteenth birthday, an ancient Coors Lite patch stitched on the brim in between a patch for last year's ESPN Extreme Sports Games in Colorado and one advertising the bungee jumping finals in South America.

The press still referred to him as a cowboy because of his do-anything attitude and I-don't-give-a-damn look. Rance was an ex-pro football player who now owned a chain of extreme sporting good stores and still made headlines with his passion for the outrageous. He'd done everything from surfing killer waves off the Australian coast to snake wrangling in the Amazon rainforest.

He looked like he always did whenever Mason saw him in person or caught a glimpse of him on the nightly news. His hat was tipped back to reveal a twinkling pair of whiskey-colored eyes and an easy grin. He wore his signature Hawaiian print unbuttoned, a white T-shirt advertising Jim Beam Whiskey beneath. His shorts were long and frayed down around the edges and he had on his favorite pair of blue flip-flops.

Make that one flip-flop.

Mason's gaze drank in the white cast that covered Rance's left leg. The hem of his shorts had been split to accommodate the bulky plaster that extended from the middle of his foot, clear up to his midthigh.

"Tell me there's an actual leg under there and some alligator didn't take a bite out of you."

"I never actually made it to the Outback. I was climbing the steps to board the plane in Austin and the damned thing wasn't locked into place. The steps slid and I fell.

"Were you on the bottom step going up to the plane, or the top step walking in?"

"I broke my leg in three places. Does that say bottom step?"

"Aw, hell, man." Mason sank down in the chair opposite his brother. "Are you okay?"

"I will be." Rance pushed his hat back even further and ran a hand over his face. "In about six weeks if all goes well. Until then, I'm supposed to take it easy."

"You don't take it easy."

"That's what I told the doc. He said if I want to walk again, I'd better get the ants out of my pants and settle down until everything heals."

"Otherwise?"

"No more gator wrestling. Or hiking in the Himalayas or anything else I've got planned."

"Sounds serious."

"Not as long as I follow his instructions, which I intend to do."

"Which is why you came home." Mason gave him a knowing look. "Couldn't resist the call of that rock wall you installed last year to practice your mountain climbing?"

Rance shrugged. "I've never been good when it comes to temptation. I figured I'd hole up here, watch the grass grow, fill up on Aunt Lurline's cooking and see for myself if my oldest brother's lost his mind." He shook his head and Mason read the same disbelief he'd felt when he'd heard the news. "Josh is really getting married?"

"That's the plan."

"Is she pregnant?"

"She doesn't have to be. He's in love."

"You really believe that?"

"I didn't believe it until I saw him. He's different now. There's this light in his eyes whenever he talks about her. Or looks at her."

"Maybe he's sick."

"He's not sick."

"He could be. I caught a bug over in the Polynesian islands during a windsurfing championship two years ago—nothing serious, just a temporary thing—and it made me act crazier than a hornet at an annual Honeyfest. I don't remember much, but when the fever peaked, I recall running around the beach, telling everyone that I was Steve Irwin, the Crocodile Hunter. Hell, I don't even like the guy. Talk about crazy."

"He's not sick. He's in love," Mason heard himself say. Love? Sure, he believed in the concept. There was too much fuss about it for it not to exist. He just didn't think it had a damned thing to do with marriage and happily ever after. Getting along with someone was all about connecting on a physical and emotional level. Then again, he supposed if he had that dual connection with someone, he'd probably fall in love with them.

But Holly Farraday didn't know the first thing about flying. She was raised in the city. Several of them, or so Josh had told him. She'd been in and out of foster homes most of her life, while Josh had grown up in the same house, on the same spread, surrounded by the same people day in and day out. She'd never set a horse or roped a calf, while he'd excelled at both. She didn't have anything in common with Josh.

And he loved her anyway. So the lust factor must be pretty high.

"He's really hot for her," Rance said as if reading Mason's mind. What he didn't say—and what both were obviously thinking—is that Josh had been hot for women in the past and he'd never gone so far as to drop down on one knee and propose. "It'll fade before they make it to the alter."

"Hopefully, not that we're going to say as much to him. This is his call, not ours."

"You don't have to remind me. I've already got a broken leg. I'm not adding a nose to the list."

Mason smiled at the memory of Josh and Rance rolling around in the pasture. They'd been thirteen and Josh had announced that he was going to kiss Mary Jean Brenton. Rance had said he shouldn't because she smelled like milk on account of she had to milk her daddy's cows before school. Josh had said he liked milk, Rance had called him a cow lover, and the fight had started. Josh had won and set the precedent when it came to women—namely the McGraw triplets respected each other's tastes and kept their mouths shut.

Josh was a grown man and he could make his own decisions.

Good and bad.

"So you're here for six weeks, huh?" Mason asked his brother.

Rance nodded. "Until my appointment with my doctor in Austin at the end of next month."

Mason noted the suitcase sitting on the porch. "Does anybody even know you're here?"

He shook his head. "I had a cab drop me off about a half hour ago. I was going to go inside, but it sounded too quiet so I thought maybe Aunt Lurline and Uncle Eustess were already in bed."

"I should be so lucky."

Rance grinned. "They're still fighting, huh?"

"Do they ever stop?"

As if on cue, a door slammed somewhere inside the house and both men listened to the sound of footsteps coming toward them. The light flipped on in the kitchen just to the right and a woman's soft hum carried on the night breeze.

"Lurline sounds pretty mellow to me."

Only because Eustess hadn't followed her out, both men realized a few seconds later when more footsteps sounded and a man cleared his throat.

"Do you have to make all those nasty sounds, Eustess? I came out here to get myself a snack and you're making me lose my appetite."

"I've got a frog in my throat."

"There's no such thing."

"There damn sure is, woman. My daddy had a

frog in his throat and I've got one in mine." He made a big show of clearing his throat and gagging several times. "See there? You can hear it."

"Unfortunately. Why, now I don't even want to eat my cream of wheat."

"Cream of wheat's too fattening anyway. You ought to try bran flakes."

"Are you saying I'm fat?"

"They don't call that thing you're wearing a housedress for nothing."

"Why, I never…"

Rance pushed to his feet. "I guess it's time I go in and give them a distraction."

"You need some help?"

"I wrestle gators, bro. I can handle a little old suitcase." He reached for his crutches, propped them under his arms and leaned to the side to retrieve his suitcase. The crutches wobbled and he would have teetered to the side if Mason hadn't caught him.

"Leave the suitcase wrestling to me. Doctor's orders."

Rance frowned and headed for the back door while Mason retrieved his bag. He was just about to pull open the screen when he turned toward Mason. "You're not going to tell anyone that I'm here, are you? Anyone in town, that is?"

"If you're referring to a certain Nadine Codge, I haven't even seen her since I've been home."

"You don't have to see her to know she's here

somewhere. She's always here. Watching and listening. I swear she has bionic hearing."

"It's called a small town. News travels fast."

"Not this news. Just pretend like I'm not here and tell Josh to do the same."

"You really think she'll come running after you like she used to?"

"You really think she won't?" Rance asked.

Mason's mind rushed back to their teenage years. Mason and his brothers had been pursued by many women in high school, but Nadine "Deanie" Codge had given new meaning to the word.

She'd been the youngest of five children and the only girl. The runt, or so everyone had always called her, hence the name Teeny Deanie. But there'd been nothing small about the way she'd hounded Rance, always showing up wherever he went and following him around, bringing him cookies. She'd wanted him to like her and the only thing he'd ever felt had been annoyance.

And a little fear.

For someone so tiny, she'd been damned persistent.

"I won't say a word," Mason told his brother. "And neither will Josh."

"Good. The last thing I need is Deanie bugging me while I'm trying to recuperate. I'm supposed to take it easy, not break my other leg trying to get away from a crazy woman. I swear, she drives me nuts."

Mason knew the feeling, only the source of his

anxiety had nothing to do with a pint-sized brunette with a gallon-sized will and everything to do with the elderly couple *this* close to duking it out in his kitchen. Not to mention a certain uptight blonde…

"Dadblame it, Eustess!" Lurline's voice grew louder as Mason followed his brother into the house. "You know I cain't stand bananas in my cream of wheat. I like raisins."

"Nobody in their right mind likes raisins. Ain't nothing better than a banana. Why, I been eating bananas all my life and my mind's as fit as ever. Did the crosswords in this mornin's paper in fifteen minutes flat."

"Are you saying I'm crazy?"

"Well, you ain't exactly the sharpest knife in the drawer. Otherwise, you'd do a few crosswords yourself 'stead of watching so much dadblamed TV."

"You watch TV."

"Sure enough. Informative shows like the news and *Jerry Springer*. I don't waste my time on *Oprah*."

"Oprah is brilliant."

"She's a Jerry wannabe…"

Obviously the first session with Charlene hadn't helped his great-aunt and -uncle. Not that he'd expected results after just an hour. Sure, he'd hoped. Especially when he'd picked them both up at Charlene's office and they'd been smiling at each other.

As if all had been right with the world.

But Eustess and Lurline had been arguing much too

long to turn it all off just like that. They'd been going at it for almost as long as Mason could remember.

Almost.

But there were a few bits and pieces of the past—other than when he'd picked them up at Charlene's place—when they'd actually seemed to like each other. He could distinctly remember Lurline feeding Eustess a bite of cherry cobbler at the annual Romeo Rodeo Bake-Off, and Eustess twirling Lurline around a sawdust-covered dance floor at the Spring Fling. Mason had been a small boy back then. Eustess had had all of his hair and a twinkle in his blue eyes and Lurline had been trim and vivacious despite birthing three kids.

But then she'd gone on to have several more, her figure had disappeared completely and Eustess had started to lose his hair. Their physical attraction to each other had obviously faded. They'd been arguing and making each other miserable ever since.

Mason knew they just needed to recapture the lust they'd initially felt. Sure, they were old. But he was a firm believer in the power of lust. Mason had seen it firsthand with Tucker and Linda who'd been total opposites, and it seemed the same way for Josh and Holly. He knew he could see it again with his great-aunt and -uncle who'd simply grown apart.

Unfortunately, Charlene Singer wasn't nearly as enlightened. She wanted a soul mate, for crying out loud. A boring, eyebrow burning pediatrician who—

Mason had heard just that afternoon from Skeeter and his cronies down at the diner—ate actual cockroaches as a form of weight control.

Talk about crazy.

On top of it all, Mason had agreed to help her.

Talk about *really* crazy.

And the real kicker was, he was actually going to go through with the ridiculous three-point plan. He'd given his word, after all, and Mason was a man who always kept his promises.

Both to others, and to himself.

7

MASON STARED at Charlene as she exited the dressing room of the elite boutique located in the heart of downtown Romeo and the air caught in his chest.

She wore a hot pink miniskirt that emphasized her endless legs and a matching halter top that hugged her breasts and outlined her ripe nipples.

More than anything, however, it was the uncertainty in her expression that made him want to reach out and pull her into his arms. It was the same look she'd worn when he'd walked in on her in the *Hee Haw* underpants. And his reaction was the same.

He didn't act on it now any more than he had then. For different reasons. He hadn't understood the pull between them back then. He'd been young and naive, and then when he'd come to understand his infatuation with her, he hadn't been able to act on it. His parents had died and his life had turned upside down. He'd had to leave, to throw himself into his rodeoing and then his business so that he didn't feel the loss as deeply.

Everything had changed now.

Yet nothing had changed because Mason was still holding back. For different reasons, of course. Charlene wouldn't welcome his advances because she didn't believe in them. She didn't believe in lust.

Unfortunately, he was stuck smack-dab in the middle of it.

She turned in a circle before giving him a questioning gaze. "How does this look?"

"Fine," he managed to say in a calm, cool voice that didn't betray the damned urge to haul her close and convince her just how fine she truly was.

"I don't know." She seemed almost disappointed by his reaction as she turned toward the floor-length mirror situated just to the right of the dressing room doorway. As if she'd expected more of a reaction. As if she wanted one.

"Maybe the color is a little too bright," she said.

"It's fine." Where the hell did that come from? He had a whole bunch of adjectives swirling in his brain—sexy, hot, bold, provocative—but damned if they could make the trek to his mouth.

"Maybe I should try the blue dress."

"Fine." He swallowed and tried to calm his pounding heart as she disappeared back behind the floor-length black curtain.

Pounding, of all things when he'd sworn to himself just that morning that he was going to focus on helping her pick out some nice clothes. He wasn't going to focus on her, as in the way the pink played up her creamy complexion or the way the spandex clung to her curves and made her seem that much more voluptuous. He wasn't going to go after a woman who wanted someone else.

Stewart.

What woman in their right mind would want a guy named Stewart? Why, the guy couldn't even use a bunson burner for Christ's sake. Sure, that had been a long time ago, but Mason wasn't going to risk getting too close. A guy didn't just outgrow that kind of clumsiness. He couldn't imagine that Charlene—smart, intelligent, sexy Charlene—would get within five feet of the guy much less want to be his soul mate.

He fought down a wave of jealousy and shifted his attention to the racks of clothing that filled the shop.

Miss Jolie's carried everything from trendy hip-hugger jeans and camisole tops to the latest in sexy underwear and do-me shoes. The shop tended to lean toward the risqué, but then Miss Jolie herself had defined the word back in her day.

She was pushing seventy-six now, but way back when, she'd worked for the notorious Red Rose Farraday who'd owned and operated one of the most famous brothels in Texas history. Jolie had been one of her most popular girls. When the place had closed down, Jolie had moved to town and opened up shop. The citizens had snubbed her at first, but as the times had changed, so had everyone's opinion of Rose and her girls.

Miss Jolie's had become the *it* place for the man-hunting Juliets, as well as every other woman in town looking to spice up her appearance.

Old Stewart would probably break out in hives if he set foot inside Miss Jolie's.

His gaze went to the old woman who stood near the front of the store, near a large glass accessory case. He watched as she pulled out a rhinestone necklace and set it on the glass counter for the customer in front of her. Her gaze caught Mason's and her face crinkled as she smiled at him.

"You just let me know if y'all need anything," she called out. "I'm always busy during the lunch hour, but I'll be back there to help just as quick as I can."

He grinned. "We're fine." There was that *fine* again.

The bell rang and Miss Jolie turned her smile to the next customer who walked in, while Mason shifted his attention to a rack of tank tops. A camouflage pattern caught his eye and he pulled it free.

"What about this?" Charlene's voice drew him around.

He turned to see her wearing a deep blue dress with a plunging neckline that went so low he expected to see her belly button peeking out at him. The material barely concealed her breasts, leaving a massive display of cleavage that made it hard to swallow. Blue outlined her hips and fell to midthigh, leaving a delicious expanse of bare legs that made his mouth water.

Oddly enough, it wasn't the scanty dress that

stopped his heart in that next instant. It was the desire that sparked deep in her eyes when his gaze collided with hers.

Heat fired in his groin and rolled through his body until he could barely breathe. He'd had chemistry with women before, but this gave new meaning to the word. It was more powerful and consuming than anything he'd ever felt, and it convinced him even more that he and Charlene should get together.

She drew a deep breath, her chest lifted, her breasts trembled, and need knifed through him. The feeling cut him to the quick and it was all he could do not to cross the few feet of distance separating them, push her up against the nearest wall and plunge fast and sure into her hot body.

And why not?

Because she isn't likely to assume the position, buddy. She doesn't believe in lust, remember? She's looking for a deeper, more meaningful connection. That's what this whole transformation is all about. She wants to prove her theory once and for all.

Or disprove it.

The thought struck and suddenly Mason felt like the biggest ass in the world. Here he was lusting after her, wanting her and wishing that she wanted him, when all he really had to do was help her.

Mason didn't believe for two seconds that Stewart was Charlene's soul mate. He had no doubt that the guy would run screaming the other way if he was faced with a drop-dead gorgeous, aggressive, daring woman. And when he did, Charlene would have to accept the truth—her theory was wrong. It wasn't similar personalities that drew and kept a couple together for the long-term. It was the physical attraction.

"We can't keep our hands off each other."

Tucker's words echoed again in Mason's head and his heart started to pound. Yep, when Charlene turned Stewart off with her new appearance, she would have proof beyond a doubt that physical attraction was all that really mattered.

Then she would stop denying the pull between her and Mason and realize that they were meant to be together. Lust mates rather than soul mates.

In the meantime, he intended to keep the chemistry sizzling and show her just how hot things could get.

"What do you think?" she asked again, uncertainty bright in her eyes.

He itched to reach out, to touch her cheek and trace the hollow beneath her eye and feel the tickle of her lashes against the pad of his finger. "It's good," he said instead, his voice gruff.

She frowned as if the response hadn't been what she'd hoped for. "Better than the pink?"

Where he'd been so damned intent on looking anywhere—everywhere—but at her since they'd walked into Miss Jolie's, he indulged himself this time. He started at the top of her head and moved down, pausing at all the interesting spots in between.

The curve of her jaw. The smooth line of her neck. The slope of her breast. The indentation of her waist. The flare of her hips. "Maybe," he finally said.

"Maybe?" Her frown deepened. "Either it is or it isn't."

He hooked the camouflage tank top back on the rack and stepped toward her. He stopped just inches shy, planted his hands on his hips and studied her, as if thinking long and hard on the subject. "I think I need a second look," he finally said. He motioned to the dressing room. "Try the other one on."

"Again?"

He grinned, slow and sure, and watched her flush. "Again."

AND THEY SAID women couldn't make up their minds?

Charlene shook her head and took off the blue dress. Pulling it right side out, she slipped it onto the hanger and hooked it on the wall. She was just about to reach for the pink when she heard the rustle of curtains, followed by a deep, husky voice.

"I like it."

Excitement rushed through her for several fast and furious heartbeats before two all-important facts registered.

First, Mason McGraw was here, now, looking at her while she wore nothing but her underwear.

Second, Mason McGraw was here, *now,* looking at her while she wore *nothing* but her *underwear.*

This was *not* happening.

She blinked, praying that he would disappear. He wasn't real. This was just a figment of her imagination. Another fantasy to add to the long list that haunted her each and every night.

He didn't disappear.

The curtains swished closed behind him and he simply stood there. He looked so tall, dark and delicious in a black T-shirt and worn, faded Wranglers, the hems frayed around his scuffed boots. He'd left his hat sitting on the dash of his truck and so there was nothing except a thick fringe of black lashes shadowing the intense green gaze that swept from her head to her toes and back up again.

Her heart thundered and goose bumps chased up and down her bare arms. *Bare*, as in *naked*. She was naked in front of a man. And not just any man. She was naked in front of Mason McGraw.

Knock, knock? You're wearing underwear, for heaven's sake. Granted, it's a pair of skimpy bikini briefs, but it could be worse.

You could be wearing a next-to-nothing thong.

Or the Hee Haw *underpants.*

The last thought killed some of the panic she was feeling and she drew a deep, calming breath. She wasn't completely nude, and she certainly wasn't the same vulnerable kid who'd run crying from her first boy/girl party after getting caught in her godawful underpants.

She could handle this.

She could handle him.

She reached for the pink halter top and pulled it to her, using the material to effectively cover her breasts as she made short work of pulling the strappy pink number from the hanger.

"I like it," he said again as he took a step toward her.

"I'm not wearing it yet," she responded as she set the hanger to the side with one hand while clutching the halter top in front of her with the other.

"That's the part I like." He took another step.

"We're supposed to be picking out the most flattering outfit," she reminded him as she turned toward the mirror, putting her back to him as she busied herself finding the hem of the halter top. "I can't very well prance around in front of everyone like this."

"Not everyone. Just me." The deep, husky words echoed in her head and thrummed through her body. He stood even closer now, his body warm and enticing in the frigid air-conditioning of the dressing room.

Okay, so maybe she couldn't handle this, Charlene admitted to herself when he stepped up behind her, her back kissing his chest.

The scent of him surrounded her and his hard warmth teased her shoulder blades. When she felt his large, calloused fingers at her waist, her fingers went limp and the halter top slipped from her hands. Her head snapped up and her gaze collided with his in the mirror.

His dark green gaze glittered back at her, bright and hot and mesmerizing. "You're really something, you know that?"

"I..." She swallowed. "You shouldn't be in here."

"No, I shouldn't." His hand slid around her waist and trailed down her abdomen to her panties. His fingers skimmed the white cotton triangle covering her sex. "I should be in *here*."

"I..." She started to say something, but his intimate touch stalled her frantic thoughts before she could come up with something coherent. Reason fled in the face of so much sensation and the only thing she could do was *feel*.

His fingertips burning through the thin material of her panties. His hard pelvis pressed against her buttocks. His strong arms surrounding her. His warm breath ruffling the hair at her temple.

"I can't stop thinking about you," he murmured.

"Me?" A rush of joy went through her before she reminded herself that she didn't care if Mason thought about her. She thought about him, in her fantasies, that is, and that was enough.

That's the way it had always been.

The way it would always be because he was hot, hunky Mason McGraw and she was Charlie Horse Singer.

"I don't think this is a good idea," she managed

to whisper, despite the sudden excitement pulsing through her veins.

"Actually, it's the best notion I've had in a long time. I want you."

Thanks to a hot pink halter top and a miniskirt.

But that was just a costume. Part of the transformation. A disguise to make her appear the daring diva she'd always wanted to be.

"And I'm getting the feeling that you want me," he continued. His fingers slid lower, to the damp cotton between her legs.

"I don't do gratuitous sex."

"Neither do I." At her wide-eyed look, he added. "Not anymore."

"Are you trying to say that you actually *like* me?"

"I'm saying that I want you."

"That's not enough of a reason to have sex."

"Isn't it the only reason? It's all about want, Charlene."

"Says you."

"This fire between us... It's not going to burn out on its own, you know. We'll have to take care of it. Even then, it's not going to completely die out. It'll flare up again and again. That's what a fire like ours does. There's no sense resisting it. We have to accept it. Manage it. Together."

"I can't."

"Or you won't?"

"Both."

"You don't have any obligation to Stewart. You two aren't even a couple."

"We're going to be."

"And I'm going to be eighty years old someday, but I'm not anywhere close to that right now. And neither are you. You aren't obligated to him, Charlie. You aren't obligated to anyone."

It was true. It had been true her entire life. She'd always been alone. Lonely. She'd been Charlie Horse Singer and despite the years that had passed, she was still no better off than when she'd been a gawky, unattractive kid. Deep inside, she knew that. Yet there was just something about hearing him point out that fact that sent a burst of anger through her. "Maybe I just don't want to sleep with you."

Hurt flashed in his gaze before his expression closed. He arched an eyebrow. "Is that so?"

"I realize that you're used to snapping your fingers and having every woman within a ten mile radius respond. But I'm not one of them."

Sure, she'd wanted to be one, had always wanted to be one, but he didn't know that. And she intended to keep it that way, which meant keeping her lustful thoughts to herself.

While Mason offered her her most wicked fantasy, he would never be her reality. He couldn't.

And that's what she wanted at this point in her life. She wanted a *real* someone. A body to keep her warm at night, to comfort her after a long day. A man to wake up to, and one who wanted to wake up to her, even though she looked like hell in the morning and slept in a rather unattractive, but comfortable, pair of pink sweat socks. A man who would have looked past a pair of *Hee Haw* panties and seen the sensitive, caring person beneath them. One who would have said hello to her in the hallway at school and not stared past her as if she hadn't existed.

A man who really and truly liked her.

A soul mate.

"I'm just not interested," she told him.

"Is that so?" Mason arched an eyebrow at her.

"That's so."

"We'll see about that, sugar." His grin was slow and knowing, and despite her decision not to have sex with him, anticipation rushed through her. "We'll just see about that."

8

"It's good to see you both again." Charlene said to the couple waiting for her in her office, as she set her cup of coffee on the coffee table, sank down into her leather chair and tried to gather her thoughts. It was barely eight a.m. on Friday. The day after Thursday. The day after what she now referred to as "the dressing room incident."

She remembered the warm press of Mason's lips on her bare neck, the feel of his hot palms cupping her breasts and her nipples pebbled. Heat rolled through her and she damned herself for opting for a steaming cup of coffee when what she really needed was a snow cone.

Charlene drew in a deep breath and forced the memory aside, the way she'd been doing over and over again for the past twelve hours.

He'd touched her.

Not just any old touch, but a familiar, I-want-to-peel-your-clothes-off-and-get-naked-and-sweaty-with-you touch.

Then again, he certainly hadn't been anxious to

peel off her clothes. There hadn't been any clothes to peel away, except a skimpy pair of panties. She'd been practically naked.

Her cheeks fired and she leaned to the side to press the intercom for the outer office. "Could you turn the thermostat down in here?" she asked Marge. "We're all but melting."

"Are you crazy?" Marge's voice crackled over the line. "My teeth are chattering."

"Then you need a better denture cream. I'm dying in here."

"Very funny. If this doctor business ever gets old, you should do stand-up. This town needs a good comedian. Why, I haven't heard a decent joke since old Morty Simcox kicked the bucket last year. That man was a scream."

"I'm serious. I really am hot."

"And *In Style*'s beating down my door for an interview." Her voice softened. "You're not sick are you? Because I only get hot flashes when I've got a fever. Then again, I also get 'em when I'm horny. Say, you're not—"

"You can have an extra hour for lunch," Charlene blurted, eager to kill Marge's speculation.

"I'm walking to the thermostat right now."

Charlene released the button and smiled at the couple that sat directly across from her on the beige leather sofa.

Eustess and Lurline McGraw.

Thankfully, Mason had dropped off his great-aunt and -uncle and left to run some errands. Charlene wasn't sure she would have been able to concentrate with him sitting in the outer office. Not with the day being so hot and the memory so fresh and... He'd *touched* her, of all things.

Not that a man had never touched her, mind you. She'd had her share of men.

Okay, so she'd had a smaller share than some, but she'd still had men. As in sex. As in she'd had enough not to get freaked out just because a man touched her in a sexual way.

It was the fact that *Mason McGraw* had done the touching.

He wasn't supposed to touch her. Not in real life. He'd never thought of her like that. He'd never thought of her at all.

She wasn't his type.

Then again, she had been wearing a teeny, tiny blue spandex dress typical of his type. And she'd looked semi-good in it. It only made sense that he might forget that she wasn't his type and make a move.

He wasn't actually attracted to *her.* It was the image.

Which meant the transformation was working. She was morphing into a daring diva, all right. On the outside, that is.

The notion should have made her feel good. Instead, it sent a rush of disappointment through her. Before she could dwell on the strange reaction, the air conditioner kicked on and a cool breeze rushed from the overhead vent, giving her a small measure of relief.

She forced aside all thoughts of Mason and concentrated on the matter at hand. "It's good to see you both for a second session."

"Glad to be here, Doc." Lurline Ketchum smiled, her weathered face scrunching into a mass of wrinkles. She wore red polyester pants, a white short-sleeved shell with large red polka dots and white leather sandals that matched the oversized handbag she clutched in her lap.

Eustess sat next to her in blue jean overalls, a white long-sleeved button-up shirt underneath. What few strands of hair he had had been slicked and combed to the side. He wore spectacles and his lips pursed as if he'd just eaten a can of homemade pickles.

"Ain't we, Eustess?" Lurline asked, elbowing her husband.

"Cain't say as I see why we need to sit here like a couple of lab rats—ouch." Eustess McGraw rubbed his side when she jabbed a little too vigorously and glared at his wife. "As thankful as a turkey on Thanksgiving," he added. Another jab to his ribs and he stiffened. "That is, um, Easter."

"We always have ham on Easter," Lurline explained. "Never turkey, so you can see why a turkey would be mighty happy. Which we are. To be here, that is."

"I see." Okay, so the only thing she saw were two people who looked as if they would rather be eating nails than sitting on her couch, but she wasn't going to say as much. Looks could be deceiving. "So—" She took a sip of her coffee and gave the old couple an easy smile. "Have you two been practicing the exercises that I gave you?"

"We sure have. Every day I tell Eustess one thing I like about him and he tells me something he likes about me. Just like you said. You're a genius, Doc."

"That's flattering, Lurline, but I'm afraid I'm not the genius. I merely give a few suggestions to help a couple work through their own difficulties. It's their feelings for each other that drive the reconnection."

"Well, it worked. Why, we ain't even close to arguing. We're cured, Doc. We ain't had an argument in a good while. Ain't that right, Eustess?"

"Not for a whole two hours."

"He means two days," Lurline interrupted. "Don't you, Eustess? Not that we actually argued two days ago. It was more like a pleasant disagreement. Ain't that right, Eustess?"

"Pleasant as pettin' a porcupine."

"He's just joking," Lurline added. "He likes to joke even when it ain't funny. Which it ain't." She reached out to pinch him. Then, as if she'd realized what she'd been about to do, she patted his arm instead and forced a smile. "I just love a man with a sense of humor."

"I'm pleased that you had a productive week, but the compliments are just the first phase of the therapy. We have a lot of work ahead of us."

"Dadblame it, Lurline. I ain't comin' here again—ouch!"

"What Eustess means is that he isn't coming here again with the same mindset. We're changed folks, Doc, just like Mason wants. And if it takes more therapy to prove it, then we're happy to oblige. Isn't that right, Eustess?"

"I ain't going to—yikes!" He rubbed his arm again where it rested next to his wife.

"Isn't that right, *Eustess*," Lurline said again, her lips drawn in a tight smile.

They stared each other down for several moments, a stand-off that Charlene was certain would erupt in a full-fledged battle. She was just about to reach for the intercom and call for backup when Eustess shrugged.

"Oh, all right," the old man grumbled.

Lurline's face crinkled in a smile as she turned toward Charlene. "So what do we have to do next?"

"Before we move on to a new exercise, I'd like to backtrack over this past week and talk about some of the compliments that came up. Eustess—" She turned toward the older man. "Why don't you tell me a few of the things you said to Lurline."

"Hells bells, why do I have to be the one to go— *argghhh*." He rubbed at his shin and Charlene blinked. Had Lurline actually kicked him? She hadn't seen the woman move. Then again, she hadn't been looking below shoulder level.

"Fine, fine," Eustess said. "I'll go first." He rubbed a few more seconds before he leaned back in his seat. "See, I told her that she… That I… That we…" His words faded into a hacking cough. "Allergies," he croaked before coughing again. He cleared his throat several times before reaching for the water glass that sat on the coffee table in front of him.

"He said I looked real pretty in my red housedress," Lurline said while he downed half the glass. "He loves it when I wear my housedresses." Eustess choked on his mouthful and Lurline swatted him on the back so forcefully that he lunged forward and nearly nose-dived into the coffee table. "Isn't that right, Eustess?"

"Ugh, yes. Yessirree." Eustess nodded as if his life depended on it. "Ain't nothin' more attractive than a housedress."

"Except for my pink sponge rollers. He said I remind him of that pretty Princess Leah from that there *Star Wars* movie when I go to bed with my rollers. On account of I roll primarily on the sides. Ain't that right, Eustess?" Before he could reply, Lurline added, "Said the likeness is downright scary."

"Scary's definitely the word when it comes to those rollers—ugh." He sucked in a sharp breath and rubbed at his thigh where Lurline's hand had been resting. "It's like watching the movie all over again."

"That's…nice," Charlene said. *At least I think so.*

She eyed the old couple and noted the belligerent set to Eustess' jaw and the guarded expression in Lurline's gaze.

They looked anything but a couple eager to reconnect with one another. Then again, they were here.

Charlene pushed aside her suspicions and smiled. "What about you, Lurline? What things did you say to Eustess?"

"Well, I told him how handsome he looked when he put on his red suspenders and his matching bow tie to take me dancing."

"But I didn't—" Eustess stuttered, but Lurline rolled right over his statement.

"And how graceful he was when we waltzed. And what a fantastic bingo player he was."

"We ain't been to bingo in over ten years."

"Lurline?" Charlene turned a questioning gaze on the woman.

"That's true, but when we used to go to bingo, he was a fantastic player and the other night I was watching the bingo play-offs on ESPN and they had this older gentleman who was the spitting image of Eustess. It reminded me of how wonderful he was and so I told him so."

Eustess arched a bushy gray eyebrow. "You did?"

"Of course I did. His memory's short," she told Charlene.

"My memory ain't no such thing. The only thing short is your brother, Monty."

"My brother is not short. He's just not as tall as everyone else."

"Which makes him short. And since he gained all of that weight and fattened himself up, he looks like one of them Weebles that the grandbabies are always playing with."

"My brother does not look like a Weeble, nor is he fat. He's stout."

"And short."

"And you're obnoxious."

"Ain't nothin' more obnoxious than you in your red housedress."

"Red is my color. The lady at the mall over in Austin said so."

"About a hundred years ago, which is how old that blasted dress is. It was an eyesore way back when and it ain't much better now—"

"A fifteen minute conversation," Charlene blurted, eager to kill the sudden tension in the room and get everyone back on track. Both pairs of eyes turned on her. "Every day for the next week. You can talk about anything, except each other. In other words, no picking faults or complaining." When they both looked as if she'd taken away their favorite toys, she added, "Talk about the weather or current events."

"We're in the middle of a dadblasted heatwave," Eustess grumbled. "There ain't nothing to talk about 'cept how hot it is and we did that weeks ago when it first started."

"Not to mention, I'm cold-natured," Lurline added. "So I think the weather's just fine."

"And everybody knows it ain't," Eustess chimed in. "So's we always get into a fight about it 'cause everybody in their right mind knows it's dadblamed hot as hell outside."

"Which means he's saying I ain't in my right mind—which I am—which constitutes fighting and we don't fight anymore. Ain't that right, Eustess?"

"There's always current events," Charlene offered.

Silence settled in for a long moment before Lurline shrugged. "They are building a new self-serve car wash on the east side of town. One of them fancy places with the air freshener gun so's you can make your car smell like pina coladas or real lemons."

"There you go," Charlene said. "I'm sure you each have your own thoughts about the car wash. What I want you to do is share them with each other. This week is all about seeing your partner in a new light. It's about rekindling the admiration and respect that you once had for each other."

"I sort of like the idea of a new car wash. Piggy's gas station over on Main will wash and wax for you, but they don't have no fancy air freshening guns."

"It's a dadblamed waste of water if you ask me. Why, when I was growing up, I washed my truck whenever it rained."

"That's the silliest thing I ever heard." As if she'd

just realized what she said, Lurline caught her lip. "Silly, but smart," she amended. "Very smart. Why, I never knew what a devoted conservationist you were, Eustess."

"If you would listen instead of doing so much yapping—"

"No picking faults," Charlene reminded the old man.

"Why, I'm just statin' the God's awful truth."

"I do tend to yap," Lurline said, despite the sparks that blazed in her eyes.

Eustess actually looked startled by the admission. He stared at his wife and she stared at him, and Charlene could have sworn a silent warning passed between them. And just to make sure that Eustess got the message, Lurline rested her hand on his thigh and curled her fingers into his flesh.

"You yap, but it's a good yap," Eustess finally said as he pried his wife's hand loose and glared at her.

"See?" Lurline turned toward Charlene. "Eustess already admires my yapping. Why, you are a genius, Doc. Why, I bet by the next session, we'll be cured."

Judging by the death grip that Lurline had on the old man's thigh, Charlene wasn't placing any bets. But when she watched them climb into Mason's truck a half-hour later, she changed her mind. Eustess held his wife's hand and helped her inside. She smiled at him. He smiled at her. They looked happy.

Maybe the therapy was working.

Her gaze shifted to the man driving and their gazes

met. He grinned, the expression slow and teasing, and her stomach hollowed out. Heat swamped her and her nipples pebbled.

"I'm not sick," Charlene said to Marge as she hiked the thermostat several degrees lower. "And I'm not horny."

Yeah, right.

9

THIS WAS BAD.

Really bad.

Charlene peered past the part in the drapes and stared at the man who knocked on her front door.

Not that she hadn't envisioned Mason McGraw knocking on her door a time or two in the past. She had. But in each scenario she'd been a) dressed to the nines in a sexy dress and high heels, her hair and makeup perfect, and b) doing something really cool like waxing her Harley or singing with her band destined to be the next Creed or Nickelback.

Reality check.

She didn't own a Harley and the closest she'd come to singing was when she belted out her favorite song—high-pitched and off-key—in the shower every morning. And the only thing she was doing at the moment was clipping possible do-me hairstyles from several magazines she'd picked up at the drugstore.

As for her appearance...

She glanced down at her ragged cut-off blue jean shorts and oversized green T-shirt, the words *Romeo*

Rangers now faded and barely visible. She wore old sweat socks that slouched down around her ankles. She'd pulled her hair into a sloppy ponytail and her makeup was just a vague memory thanks to the antiwrinkle scrub she'd purchased for an outrageous amount of money on her last shopping trip into Austin.

Really bad?

More like a major disaster.

Her heart jumped and anxiety rushed through her. He couldn't see her like this. While she had no illusions that he really and truly wanted her—his interest was merely a ploy to dissuade her from her plan—she wasn't going to go out of her way to solidify the notion.

She held her breath while the knocking continued. She wasn't going to answer the door. Then he would go away and she could make up some excuse tomorrow during their lunch consultation as to why she wasn't home at seven in the evening on a work night. Especially when Romeo practically rolled up the sidewalks by five. It wasn't as if she could still be cruising the grocery store or checking out books at the library.

She closed her eyes as dread rolled through her and her heart pounded even faster. To make matters worse, her car was sitting in the driveway. She was home, end of story.

Of course, she *could* be in the shower, which was

a valid reason not to hear his knock. Or maybe she'd simply been so tired that she'd gone to bed early. Better yet, maybe she was checking in on old Mrs. Johnson who lived two houses down and had recently had cataract surgery. Then again, it was common knowledge that Mrs. Johnson went to bed at seven every night on account of she had a rooster that woke her up at daybreak every morning (along with half the neighborhood, Charlene included). She could be next door at Mrs. Owens' buying Happy Camper cookies as promised. Susie, the oldest of Mrs. Owens' five daughters, was president of Happy Campers Troop 54, and just that afternoon she'd toted home eight cases of cookies for their annual sale. While Charlene avoided the bright pink boxes like most teenagers avoided asparagus, she couldn't not support the local youth—

"Are you okay?" Mason's deep voice echoed in her ears and her eyes snapped open to find him standing in the open doorway…of the door she'd forgotten to lock. He wore faded Wranglers that clung to his muscular thighs and a soft white cotton shirt that hugged his broad shoulders. He smelled of leather and wind and a rugged masculinity that filled her nostrils and did dangerous things to her common sense. His faded straw Resistol sat tipped back on his head, his bright green gaze hooked on her. Concern glittered in the green depths and something warm unfolded in her chest.

Followed by a well of panic.

He was standing in her open doorway.

Charlene ducked behind the drapes and nearly snatched the rod off the wall in the process.

"Charlene?" Her name was a question and her panic escalated. Not only was he standing in her open doorway, but he was looking at her, talking to her, and worse, she had to answer him back.

"I…" She licked her lips and tried to draw a much needed breath that didn't include Mason's delicious scent. Fat chance. "I—I'm fine." Another breath and her body temperature rose several degrees.

"I've been knocking for five minutes. Why didn't you answer?"

"I didn't hear you."

"You're standing right next to the door."

"I am now." *Just breathe and don't think about how good he smells. Or about how close he is. Or how good he looks.* "But I haven't always been in this position. I was upstairs and I couldn't hear the knocking." Hey, it sounded good.

Mason didn't look convinced. "So what brought you downstairs?"

"I was on my way to the kitchen. Then I thought I heard a knock, so here I am at the door."

"But you still didn't answer it," he said, a knowing look in his eyes.

"You barged in before I had a chance. Speaking of which, what are you doing here?" There. Now she was the one asking questions and he could do the squirming.

Only Mason McGraw didn't squirm. He looked calm. Cool. Handsome. *Determined.*

A shiver rippled through her as she recognized the same look he'd worn in the dressing room earlier that week.

Just before he'd touched her.

Her grip tightened on the drapes she held in front of her.

"I was driving by on the way home from the feed store and I thought I would stop by."

"I'm not on your way home," she added.

"You are if I turn left on Main and circle back around town." He grinned, slow and easy, and she found herself almost mesmerized.

Her panic eased and her heart slowed and she actually felt herself smile. "That's the silliest thing I've ever heard."

"I know." His grin faded and something dark and delicious glittered in his gaze. "But it's the truth."

Her heart kicked up a beat. "Why?" The word was out before she could stop it.

"I could tell you, but then I'd have to kiss you."

"That's *kill* you."

"Not in this case."

He was so close that she had half a mind to lean forward and kiss him herself, just to cut the tension that stretched between them and satisfy the lust that pushed and pulled inside of her. A lust that had driven her to walk by his locker so many times when they'd been back in school. A lust that had always been one-sided.

Until now.

Just as the thought struck, she pushed it away. He didn't really want her. He was trying to prove a point.

She knew that, but at the same time, she couldn't stop herself from at least contemplating the notion.

That Mason really did want her. That he wanted to pull her close and kiss her deeply and carry her up to her bed or to the kitchen table or the front porch swing and make mad, passionate love to her.

She tried to push the notion away, but it lingered in her head and she heard herself say, "Why are you really here?"

Not that it mattered. She wanted happily ever after more than hot, torrid sex.

He rested one hand on the wall near where she stood in front of the window and leaned in just a fraction. Her nipples tingled in response and she swallowed.

Okay, so the desire for a happily ever after and torrid sex were running a close race at the moment. Very close. But the first would win because Charlene had learned a long time ago that banking on lust ultimately ended in heartache. Her mother and father's failed marriage proved as much.

Charlene wouldn't doom herself to the same fate

as her mother. She wouldn't spend her nights crying and her days trying to hide her misery from her child.

Forewarned was forearmed, she always said. So Charlene was making the smarter decision.

No matter how badly she wanted to kiss Mason McGraw…or press her lips to the pulse beat at the base of his throat…or peel his T-shirt up and run her hands over the hard muscles of his chest.

"You wanted my advice about hairstyles." His deep voice shattered her dangerous thoughts.

"Excuse me?"

"You asked me why I'm here. Aren't we doing the hair thing next?"

"That's tomorrow. Lunch. At the diner." With lots of people so she wouldn't be tempted to throw her beliefs to the wind and jump him.

As if he could read her mind, he grinned. "I'm afraid that's no good for me. I'm branding new calves tomorrow, so if you want me, it'll have to be tonight."

The *want me* stalled in her brain and stirred a very vivid image of Mason, naked and very aroused, spread out on her lilac colored sheets. It was one of her favorite fantasies in which she wore a slinky, sexy white see-through nightgown and had her way with him—

Her thoughts careened to a halt as she remembered that she wasn't wearing anywhere close to a sexy nightie. Her feet heated inside the beat-up sweat socks and the flush worked its way clear to her head.

"Would you, um, excuse me for a second?"

"What?"

She indicated the curtain she held in front of her. "I'm not really decent."

"You're plenty decent. Shorts. Shirt. Smacks of decency."

"These are my lounging around clothes and since you're here, I won't be lounging. I'll be visiting. So I really think I should change."

He stared at her, a puzzled look on his face. Then he shrugged. "Knock yourself out."

When he just kept looking at her, she motioned for him to turn around.

He looked surprised. "You've got to be kidding? I've already seen you."

Unfortunately. "I would really appreciate it." She didn't mean to sound so desperate, but the words came out anyway.

She half expected him to laugh at her. That's what most hot, hunky men would have done when faced with such a request. But Mason didn't so much as crack a smile. Instead, he stared at her long and hard as if searching for something before he finally shrugged again and turned.

Charlene didn't waste a precious moment. She hit the stairs running and didn't stop until she'd reached her bedroom. Leaning back against the closed door, she drew a deep breath and tried to calm her pounding heart.

Mason McGraw was really here, in the flesh, right now.

The truth galvanized her into action and she raced to the closet, straight to the new outfits she'd purchased earlier that day.

She retrieved a neon green miniskirt and skimpy white tank top and tugged them both on. Then, before she could think about how uncomfortable she felt in the revealing clothes and dive into a pair of cover-everything-up sweats, she headed back downstairs.

While she didn't feel comfortable, she couldn't very well face Mason McGraw looking like a groupie.

That would be as bad as the time she got caught in her *Hee Haw* underpants. That humiliating moment was enough for a lifetime.

Besides, if she truly intended to fool Stewart with her new appearance, she needed to get used to her new clothes.

Now was as good a time as any to start.

"Where's the birdhouse?" he asked her when she found him in the living room a few minutes later.

"Excuse me?"

He held up a book he'd pulled from her massive collection. *How To Build Your Own Birdhouse in Four Easy Steps.*

"I haven't actually built one."

"Why not?"

"I don't have the time. During the semester, it's

all I can do to eat and sleep. During the summer break, it's almost just as bad. I don't actually have classes, but there's a lot of work in preparing for the new semester."

"What about surround sound?" He held up *How To Customize Your Own Surround Sound System*.

"Not yet."

He held up another book. "Have you braided your own rug?"

"No."

"Baked homemade bread?"

"I'm afraid not."

"Made your own jelly?"

"No. I told you, I'm really busy."

"You don't do any of these things, but you read about doing them."

"I like knowing things."

"Seems pointless to me if you're never going to use the knowledge."

It did to her, too, now that she heard him say the words. A wasted effort. Like all the years she'd spent lusting after Mason McGraw while he'd paid her absolutely no attention. Like the way she'd rushed up the stairs to change just to impress him.

She dismissed the notion. The clothes weren't for him. They were for her. The woman she was transforming herself to be.

"I really wasn't expecting anyone." She busied herself gathering up the magazines that she had spread out on the coffee table. She stacked the clippings and scissors off to the side near the magazines before turning to find that Mason had shifted his attention from her bookshelf to the pictures that lined the mantel.

"Your folks?" He indicated the one and only wedding picture her mother had kept.

"Once upon a time."

"They look really happy."

"They do, don't they?" She came up beside him and studied the picture that had been sitting on the mantel for as long as Charlene could remember. "I guess that just goes to show that looks can be deceiving. One minute everything seemed fine and the next, they were getting a divorce. But then it only stands to reason. They were too different. You have to have common ground for a marriage to work."

"Is that what you teach your college students?"

"As a matter of fact, it is."

"My parents had plenty of common ground and their marriage didn't work."

"Your parents didn't get a divorce," she added.

"True. They were married right up until my mother died, but they weren't really *married*. My father cheated and my mother looked the other way. The only time they ever actually spent together was on the back of a horse." At her questioning glance, he said, "That was their common ground. The horses. The ranch. That was it." He eyed the picture of her parents, their arms wrapped around each other. "There was no fire between them."

"You think that would have made a difference?"

His deep, green gaze met hers. "I know it. It's all about the fire that burns between a man and woman. The hotter, the better. That's what keeps a marriage together."

"It didn't keep my parents together. My mother's down in Florida and my father lives in Pennsylvania. They avoid each other like the plague."

"Maybe it hurts too much to see something you can't have."

"Or maybe the fire fizzled and they just can't stand the sight of each other."

His gaze shifted back to the picture. "They definitely look like two people who can't stand each other. If they were any closer, he'd be wearing that wedding dress."

"Back then." She eyed the young couple and blinked back the sudden tears that stung her eyes. "When I was little, I remember them cuddling and kissing on the couch every night like a couple of teenagers." The memories played in her head and she smiled for a brief moment. "But then one day it just stopped. I came home to find that my dad had packed his things and left. My mother didn't seem the least bit surprised. I heard her crying that night—every night, actually, for the next few months—but for the most part, she seemed okay with it." Her throat tightened, but then she felt the warm press of Mason's fingers and she managed to swallow.

"Doesn't sound like fizzling to me," Mason said after a long moment.

"What do you mean?"

"Fizzling is something that happens slowly." He let his hand fall away from her. "One day he forgets to kiss her goodbye. The next day she stops holding his hand while they watch television. The next he stops holding the door open for her. The next she stops making his favorite dinner. They both get older and they drift apart. I think that's what happened with Aunt Lurline and Uncle Eustess. They fizzled. But in your parents' case, it sounds like their fire—" he motioned to the picture, "—got snuffed out."

The possibility lingered in her mind as Mason turned his attention to the next photograph.

Snuffed out meant something sudden and unexpected and monumental had happened, like an extramarital affair or the death of a child. Something big enough to kill the fierce attraction her parents used to have for each other. But there'd been no major event in the Singer household. One minute they'd liked each other and the next, they'd been in court claiming irreconcilable differences.

Which meant Mason McGraw didn't have a clue what he was talking about.

That's what she told herself. The trouble was, she wasn't quite sure she believed it.

"I didn't know you played for the girls' basketball team the year we went to the state play-offs." Mason's voice drew her attention from her conflicting thoughts and she stared at the framed 5x7 of a tall, awkward girl in a green Romeo Rangers basketball uniform.

"I didn't actually play. I sprained my wrist during practice. I was decent at dribbling and passing the ball, but I could never actually shoot it. Two left hands."

"What?"

"The coach said I had two left hands when it came to hitting the net. I was really awkward and uncoordinated."

"You obviously grew out of it." His gaze roamed over her and if she hadn't known better, she would have sworn she saw a glimmer of appreciation.

But she knew better. He was Mason McGraw, after all. Her fantasy.

"I'm really not prepared for the hairstyle discussion tonight." Eager to change the subject, she motioned to the coffee table and the stack of magazines and clippings. "I wanted to have at least a dozen samples to choose from."

"How many do you have?"

"Five. Look, if you're too busy tomorrow, we

could do it the following day…" she said, but he'd already settled himself on her couch.

"Five's plenty," he told her. He reached for the small stack and leafed through them.

"See anything that might work?" she finally asked, perching on the edge of an armchair on the opposite side of the coffee table. The dark cherry wood surface separated them, putting enough space between them that she was no longer overwhelmed by the warm pull of his body.

Mason stared at the samples and shook his head. "These are too high maintenance."

"That's okay. I don't mind putting in the time. I know I'll have to, if I want to make this work." When he glanced up, a questioning look on his face, she added, "You've heard of a bad hair day? For me, it's more like a bad hair decade."

He grinned. "What's wrong with your hair?"

"It's straight. Very straight. Meaning, I have to use a load of rollers and lots of hairspray to get it to look any other way but straight. It wouldn't be a problem, except I don't do rollers and hairspray very well."

"So why did you pick out these styles?"

"I figured I could take the picture over to the Hair Saloon. I'll let them fight with the rollers and hairspray."

"I hate to break it to you, but there's nothing sexy about rollers and hairspray."

"Are you trying to tell me that one of the major

requirements of being a daring diva *isn't* having a can of Aqua Net and knowing how to use it?"

He grinned. "Maybe for the wannabes in this town. But I think you need something a little different."

"As in?" *A different head,* a voice whispered. *Along with a different body.*

But even as the doubts rolled through her, she didn't believe them the way she usually did. Not with him looking at her so intently.

Wanting her.

Yeah, right. She tried to dismiss the thought, but she couldn't. Not this time.

"Real divas don't tease and spray their way to sexy." He pushed to his feet and walked around the couch.

Before she could draw her next breath, he came up behind her and his strong fingers went to the clasp of her ponytail. He tugged the fastening loose and let her hair spill down around her shoulders.

"They work with what they have." His deep voice slid into her ears. "It's about relaxing and cutting loose." He threaded his fingers through her hair and massaged her scalp. "You're not relaxed."

"No, but if you keep doing that, I'm sure I'll get there."

His laugh was warm and almost as lulling as his hands. He continued to massage her and she closed her eyes. She actually relaxed for the next few moments and forgot all about her doubts. Instead, she focused on the bubbles of warmth that rippled along her skin and the mesmerizing way he kneaded her scalp.

"There," he finally said, his deep voice pulling her back to reality long enough for her to open her eyes. "I think this works."

She pushed to her feet and walked over to the small mirror that hung on a nearby wall. Her reflection stared back at her, her pale blond hair long and unkempt, as if she'd just rolled out of bed. But even more than her hair, it was the flush to her cheeks and the brightness in her eyes that made her look sexy and wanton and…daring.

"I can promise you it won't stay this way without at least a half can of hairspray," she argued.

"Being a real diva isn't about what you look like." He came up behind her. "It's the attitude."

"I know that's part of it, but I want to get the looks and the moves—"

"Attitude is all of it," he broke in. "It's about turning loose your inhibitions and going with what you feel inside. If you want to kiss me, you should stop thinking about it and just do it."

She caught his stare in the mirror. "Who says I want to kiss you?"

"Do you?" His gaze seemed to stare straight through her, past all the doubts.

No. The lie was there in her head, but with him staring at her, into her, she couldn't seem to push it past her lips.

She shrugged. "Maybe I do, but it doesn't matter because I'm not going to."

"Then I guess I'll just have to kiss you." Before she could protest, he whirled her around and his mouth covered hers.

10

MASON'S TONGUE swept and plundered Charlene's mouth as he pulled her close. He tasted of sweet tea and warm male and...yum.

For the next few moments, she forgot her disbelief that he really and truly wanted her. He felt too hard and hot and right, and so she kissed him back.

She opened her mouth and tangled her tongue with his. Her arms curled around his neck and she pressed herself up against him.

His hands swept down to cup her bottom and rub her against the hard bulge of his jeans. "Charlie, you feel so good," he murmured against her lips. "So damned good." He kissed her again, hard and hot and deep.

His hands skimmed down her body and slid beneath her tank top. Warm fingers dipped inside her bra to cup her bare breast. He caught her nipple between two fingers and squeezed just enough to send a sharp spike of desire through her.

Raw, brazen, I-need-you-now-or-I'll-explode *desire*. The kind she'd envisioned in her fantasies. The sort they wrote about in novels and glorified on the big screen. Fiction, or so she'd thought until she'd felt it for herself.

Right now. Right this moment. *Real.*

"Knock, knock!" A woman's voice pierced the haze of pleasure that surrounded Charlene and zapped her back to reality. "Anybody home?"

"I'll be right there," she called out, grasping at the hem of her tank top which had slid up to her chest thanks to Mason's strong, purposeful hands and her momentary lapse in judgement.

He wanted her.

The realization echoed in her head and sent a rush of excitement through her, followed by a surge of nervous anxiety.

Because he wasn't some fantasy. He was the real thing. And he really wanted her.

"I—I have to go." She pulled away and rushed toward the foyer just as her neighbor, Janice Owens, pushed the front door completely open. Charlene needed to think. To understand what had just happened between them. One minute she'd been convinced he'd been putting on a show to scare her from her plan and the next—*bam*—he really wanted her, no hidden agenda required.

"Well, hello," Charlene blurted, reaching the door just in time to keep the woman from stepping inside. After all, she didn't understand what had just happened. The last thing she needed was an outsider speculating about it, as well. "So nice to see you, Mrs. Owens."

The woman tried to peer past Charlene, as if she suspected something had been keeping her from the door. Or someone. "It's about time you opened up."

"I—I'm working on a special project and I must have lost myself." Amen. "What can I, um, do for you?"

The woman gave her a knowing look and waved a pink box. "You said you'd stop by for cookies."

"I did, didn't I? It must have slipped my mind."

"No problem. We've made the rounds on the block, but we've still got plenty left. Don't we, Susie?"

Charlene's gaze darted to the pint-sized version of Janice Owens who stood just to her right.

Twelve year-old Susie wore the traditional brown and green Happy Campers uniform, complete with camouflage beret, and carried a cardboard carton brimming with pink boxes of Mint Creme Extremes, Peanut Butter Pinwheels and Chocolate Chipper Doodles.

"We've got a whole case on account of Mom ordered too much 'cause she wants to win the three day, all expense paid trip to this fancy spa that they're giving away to the leader of the troop who sells the most cookies," the child said without taking a breath.

"Now, now, Susie. The trip is just an added incentive. The real prize is all the new camping equipment the troop will be able to purchase with the proceeds." Janice smiled at Charlene. "It's all about the girls."

"Of course." Charlene drew a deep breath, grabbed her purse that hung on the coatrack just inside the doorway and retrieved her wallet. "I'll take a box of each."

"That would help tremendously." Janice motioned to Susie who handed over the boxes. "And speaking of help, isn't that Mason McGraw's truck parked in your driveway?" Janice tried to stare past Charlene. "Why, I bet he'd love to buy a few boxes and help out the girls."

"On second thought," Charlene stepped out onto the porch and pulled the door closed behind her, effectively blocking Janice's nosy stare. "Why don't I just take the whole case?"

After writing out a check for the cookies, Charlene watched Janice and Susie disappear next door. Once they were out of sight, she drew a deep breath and turned toward her front door. Her hand paused on the handle. Her heart pounded in anticipation.

Because she knew what would happen once she stepped back inside. He would step up to her, kiss her, and she would lose all rational thought.

Yeah, right.

The old, familiar doubt reared its ugly head, but it didn't ease her anxiety the way it usually did.

Mason did want her.

And if she opened the door right now, she knew she would find out exactly how much.

As much as she wanted him?

She wasn't sure. She only knew that the truth waited on the other side and she just wasn't sure if she could face it just yet.

A few frantic moments later, Charlene sank down onto the porch swing, a box of Mint Creme Extremes in her hands. Five percent mint and ninety-five percent chocolate. Which put them right up there at the top of her Hands Off list.

Right beneath Mason McGraw who'd occupied the number one spot for as long as she could remember.

The thought stirred an image of him naked and panting, over her, surrounding her, *inside* of her...

She opened the box.

The first cookie was good, but she needed great. Delicious. Decadent. *Satisfying*.

She reached for number two. And then number three.

She was on her sixth cookie when she heard the front door open.

The porch swing sat at the end of the porch, beyond the reach of the porch light and she sank back into the shadows, praying that he didn't see her during such a weak, pitiful moment. That would surely kill any lust he might actually be feeling.

A daring diva wouldn't be hiding on the front porch with a box of cookies when she had a red-hot man waiting for her inside.

"Those must be some cookies." He pulled the door

closed and stepped toward her. A few seconds later, the swing dipped as he sat down next to her.

"They're all right," she said after swallowing her mouthful and trying to calm her frantic heart. As nervous as he made her, there was something oddly comforting about his shoulder resting against hers. As if they were old friends who'd been sitting side-by-side on the swing for ages, eating cookies and listening to the crickets buzz. "Want a taste?"

"I definitely want a taste."

"Help yourself." She held out the box to him.

He took the cookies and set them aside.

"What are you doing?" she asked as he pushed to his feet. The swing bounced and shook as he turned and dropped to his knees in front of her. He reached for the waistband of her miniskirt.

"Helping myself," he murmured as he tugged her zipper down, his gaze locked with hers. There was no mistaking the heat that fired his eyes.

"But y-you can't. I mean, we're on my front porch. Someone might see." *Someone might see? What happened to You're not my soul mate, therefore this is a bad idea?*

He was her fantasy. She'd dreamt of him too many times not to indulge herself when faced with the real thing.

"You're right," he murmured. "Someone might see. Does it really matter?"

It did. She was Dr. Charlene Singer, for heaven's

sake. She preached about emotional attraction instead of physical as the foundation for any and all relationships. *And she believed what she preached.*

Or she used to.

With Mason's lips so warm against her bare skin, she wasn't so sure anymore. She only knew that she liked what he was doing to her.

"Forget about everything and everyone." He unfastened the button and shimmied the material down her legs, his fingers grazing her supersensitive skin. "It's just you and me now."

Heat swept through her and chased the oxygen from her lungs as he urged her legs apart and wedged himself between her knees. His fingertips swept from her calves, up the outside of her knees until his hands came to rest on her thighs.

"I bet you taste just as good as you feel." He touched his lips to the inside of her thigh just a few inches shy of her panties.

He nibbled and licked and worked his way slowly toward the heart of her. She found herself opening her legs even wider, begging him closer.

He trailed his tongue over the silk covering her wet heat and pushed the material into her slit until her flesh plumped on either side. He licked and nibbled at her until her entire body wound so tight she thought she would shatter at any moment. But she didn't. She couldn't. Not until she felt him completely with no barriers between them.

He gripped the edge of her panties and she lifted her hips to accommodate him. The satin material slithered down her legs and landed in a puddle near her feet.

He caught her ankles and urged her knees over his shoulders.

He slid his large hands beneath her buttocks and drew her to the edge of the swing. Dipping his head, he flicked his tongue along the seam between her slick folds in a long, slow lick that sucked the air from her lungs.

His tongue parted her and he lapped at her sensitive clit. He tasted and savored, his tongue stroking, plunging, driving her mindless until she came apart beneath him. A cry vibrated from her throat and shattered the quiet stillness surrounding them.

Her heart beat a frantic pace for the next few moments as she tried to come to terms with what had just happened.

She'd had an orgasm. A powerful, overwhelming orgasm unlike any she'd ever experienced. Thanks to Mason McGraw.

"So are you going to invite me in?" he asked her when she managed to open her eyes.

Yes! her hormones screamed.

At the same time, there was just something about the intense way he was looking at her, as if he meant to have her here and now and never, ever let her go.

"I—I really don't think we should be doing this." She tugged at her miniskirt while he pushed to his feet. She scrambled to an upright position and fought with the button at her waistband.

"You're kidding, right?"

"Not that I didn't enjoy it. I did, but I shouldn't have. You and I really aren't right for each other."

"When are you going to stop reading about life and start living it?"

"I beg your pardon?"

"You heard me." He reached for her waistband and slid the button easily into place, his gaze dark and knowing as he stared down at her. "One day you're going to have to stop hiding behind that big brain of yours and start acting on what's inside."

Before she could respond, he kissed her roughly on the lips and walked away.

And Charlene was left to wonder if she'd just made the best decision of her life, or, possibly, the worst.

MASON TIGHTENED his hands on the steering wheel and fought the urge to turn the truck around and haul ass back to Charlene's house. The taste of her lingered on his lips and his dick throbbed and…

Christ, he wanted her. He wanted her a hundred different ways, and there wasn't a damned thing he could do about it.

He wouldn't do anything about it.

He'd shown her tonight how good things could be between them, and so the next move was up to her. If his instincts were right and she did want him as much as he wanted her, she would act on her lust and take things a step further. She would come on to him, and then he would know beyond a doubt that Charlene Singer was his one and only.

And if she didn't?

Better to know now before he'd wasted any more time. Mason wasn't settling for a woman who felt anything less for him than what he felt for her.

He wanted mutual, all-consuming lust.

Mason reached the edge of town and turned left onto the farm road that would take him to the Iron Horse. He fixed his gaze on the road, but in his mind's eye, all he saw was Charlene.

Her face flushed, her eyes heavy-lidded, her lips parted on a moan. She was open and trembling in front of him, her soft pink folds glistening in the porch light.

Hunger knifed through him and he shifted on the seat to give his hard-on more room. *Right.* He was damn near bursting and there was no relief in sight.

Working at the button of his jeans, he slid the waistband open and shoved his zipper down. His erection bobbed forward, pushing against the soft cotton of his briefs. His fingers grazed the hard bulge and a gasp caught on his lips.

He wanted her, all right, more than he'd ever wanted any woman. Did she want him as much?

His dick screamed *yes!* but his brain wasn't half as sure. Maybe he was reading more into her heated looks and the longing he'd glimpsed whenever he caught her staring at him.

Maybe.

Lord knew, when it came to women, good judgment didn't run in the McGraw family.

Mason's grandfather had married a woman who'd given him a son and a hard day's work with little complaint, but nothing more.

There'd been no I-have-to-have-you-right-now-or-I'll-die lust. No hand-holding on the porch swing. No lingering glances or secretive smiles whenever they were together. Nothing even remotely resembling what he'd witnessed between Tucker and his wife.

Romeo McGraw had cheated on his own wife with the infamous Red Rose Farraday. He'd been so hot and bothered over her, so head over heels in love, that he'd actually given away hundreds of acres of the Iron Horse to her as a declaration of his feelings. A move he'd later regretted. While he'd loved Rose, she hadn't loved him in return. He'd been just another customer and she hadn't been the least bit anxious to make their relationship exclusive. Nor had she held the Iron Horse with the same reverence. She'd gone on to fragment the ranch even more by dividing up her land among her girls.

Romeo's foolishness—believing in love and acting on it—had haunted him until the day he died. He'd regretted giving up the land. More than anything else.

Josh had since bought back all of the missing pieces at the old man's dying request, but it didn't change the fact that Romeo had made a bad call.

Mason's father had used poor judgment, as well. While he'd realized early on that the land was all that mattered, he'd taken things to the opposite extreme.

Rather than giving away the land, he'd been obsessed with increasing his holdings. And to do so, he'd married a woman he hadn't been the least bit attracted to in order to expand the Iron Horse. She'd been the daughter of a neighboring rancher and her father had offered a sizeable dowry. Even more, she'd been the sole heir for the entire spread. When her parents had passed on a few years after she'd married, the Iron Horse had nearly doubled in size. The marriage had been one of convenience, nothing more. His father hadn't lusted after his mother, and she hadn't lusted after him. But unlike his father, his mother had taken her decision much more serious. She'd never been a slave to her own desire and she'd been faithful up until her death.

Meanwhile, her husband had slept with more women than there were in town.

The thing was, she hadn't really been hurt because she hadn't ever cared.

She'd been relieved. She'd told Mason as much on her deathbed. She'd suffered a surprise miscarriage—she hadn't realized she was even pregnant—and had been rushed to the hospital where she'd died the next morning from an associated infection. Mason had stayed with her while Josh had gone to look for their father who'd been out with his latest whore.

"Don't apologize for him," she'd told her son that night. "I don't blame your father. If anything, I respect the fact that he doesn't push me. Most men would make their wives comply with their needs, but not your father. He knows that I didn't marry him for that. That's why our marriage has been successful while others have ended in divorce."

Her words echoed in his head as he pulled up at the ranch house and killed the truck's engine. He sucked in his breath, tucked his package back into his pants and tried not to wince as he fastened his zipper.

Climbing out, he heard the loud voices of his great-aunt and -uncle that carried in the still night air. The sound of a football game drifted from the opposite side of the house where Rance's old bedroom was located.

Mason turned on his heel and headed for the barn. With a hard-on the size of Texas, he wasn't in any condition to face the old couple. Nor was he in any position to shoot the shit with his brother. He had too much on his mind.

Successful?

His mother had died alone and lonely. And his father had killed himself in a car accident because he couldn't stand the guilt. It was a tragedy far worse than any divorce.

Their marriage had been a mistake, and Mason and his brothers had suffered because of it. They'd not only both lost their parents in less than twenty-four hours, they'd been pushed out of their home.

But Mason was back now, and he was holding tight.

Even more, he was making the Iron Horse a real home, complete with a wife he wanted more than his next breath. One who wanted him just as much.

And so he had to let Charlene take the lead. Because he needed to know beyond a doubt that she was that woman.

In the meantime…

He stopped at the water pump situated en route to the barn. He cranked the handle and let the cool well water splash into the large wooden trough that sat beneath.

A few seconds later, he ducked his head into the water and held himself under until his lungs burned as badly as the rest of his body. He came up sputtering and gasping for air. The liquid dribbled down his neck and shoulders and cooled his heated skin.

At least up top.

Down south, however, he was still a damned sight hot. Even the next hour spent galloping at breakneck speed beneath the black, star-studded sky did little to ease his body temperature.

He soon found himself back at the watering trough. He pumped more water, ducked his head under again and tried to kill the thoughts that consumed him.

Charlie.

Under him. Surrounding him. Burning with him until the fire died down enough so that he could function again.

He came up sputtering and swiped at the water that ran into his eyes. He could only pray she didn't take too long before making her move. Otherwise, he was liable to drown himself.

11

Riding tip #8: control the penis, mentally and physically.

Charlene read the bold print on page fifteen of *How To Ride 'Em Like a Rodeo Queen* and did her best not to blush. After all, she was supposed to be an expert on man/woman relationships.

Then again, this wasn't about talking and connecting with each other. This was all about wild, wicked sex.

The kind she would have undoubtedly had last night with Mason McGraw had she not come to her senses and put a stop to things.

She'd had to stop, she reminded herself. While she had no doubt that Mason did, indeed, lust after her, lust was just not part of her plan.

And neither were cataclysmic orgasms that made her toes tingle and her tummy tremor.

Her mind rushed back to the swing and the feel of his silky hair on the insides of her thighs, his fingers burning into her bottom, holding her close as his hot, raspy tongue stroked her most sensitive spot…

Charlene shifted in her seat and tried to calm the sudden pounding of her heart.

They hadn't even had sex and she'd come like Old Faithful, her climax intense and powerful. She could only imagine what a real bonafide orgasm, with him inside of her, racing to the finish line with her, would feel like.

Too intense. Too powerful.

Too shameful, a voice whispered. She had a significant other, at least in her mind, and so she'd had to put on the brakes. At least that's the conclusion she'd come to that morning after tossing and turning all night. Her hesitation hadn't had a thing to do with her own insecurities or the fact that while Mason had made one of her fantasies come true, she wasn't nearly as confident that she could do the same for him.

Bottom line, she was a taken woman.

Taken. As in unavailable.

As in inexperienced, that same voice whispered. *You've got the equipment, you're just not sure how to use it.*

She forced aside the thought. Sex was sex. No mystery involved. She knew where everything went and she knew how to get it there.

There were, however, certain techniques that could heighten the experience. At least according to the outrageous and extremely descriptive book in front of her.

A real rodeo queen realizes that she's in charge

of the ride and she takes the lead the moment she climbs into the saddle.

In other words, she doesn't lie motionless on the porch swing while a man does all the work.

She sets the pace with the motion of her hips, be it fast or slow. She also keeps her chin up, her breasts out and proud, and gives her cowboy a stirring visual, as well as an intense ride.

Riding tip #9: Nothing says ride 'em like a great, big yee-hawwwww!

A real rodeo queen enjoys the ride and isn't the least bit shy when it comes to voicing her pleasure. She takes and gives with great relish.

Namely, she doesn't push him away just when he's about to sweep her up into his arms and move the action into the bedroom, Charlene thought.

She gasps and moans, cries and shouts, and lets her partner know exactly how much she's enjoying herself.

Riding tip #10: A real rodeo queen never climbs into the saddle without her boots on—

"The coffee machine is broken." Marge's voice cut through Charlene's concentration.

She slapped the book closed. Her head snapped up and her gaze collided with her secretary's. "What?" She did her best not to look rattled.

"The coffee machine is broken." Marge's eyes narrowed. "What are you reading there?"

Charlene leaned forward and rested her arm on the top of the book. "Just research on a new communication technique I'm thinking of trying." With her other arm, she reached out, snatched a folder from the corner of her desk and pulled it on top of the book where her arm had been. She clasped her hands in front of her and gave Marge a big smile. "So what was that about the coffee machine?"

"It's broken." Marge gave her a Hello?-Anyone-home look before shaking her head. "Which means it isn't working. Which means you can forget having any coffee until I can get over to Edmunds Appliances and buy us a new one."

"Which will be?"

"Late this afternoon. I've got a ton of notes to type up." She took a sip from a foam cup and blew out an exasperated breath.

Charlene gave her a suspicious look. "I thought you said the machine was broken."

"It is. It broke right after I managed to salvage this one cupful." She took another sip. "Boy, that hits the spot."

"You're not going to share, are you?"

"It's a really small cup."

"So what am I supposed to do?"

"You could always walk yourself over to the Fat Cow Diner and get yourself a cup to go. And while you're there, you can get me one, too, because this is going to last me all of five seconds." Marge downed the rest of her cup. "There. Now I'm going into withdrawal."

"I'll go, but I'm not carrying back three cups of coffee."

"I only want one."

"The other two are for me. If you want one, you'll have to come along."

"You're a slave driver, you know that?" Marge asked before turning to retrieve her purse.

Charlene took the opportunity to slide her new book into the back of her bottom drawer before joining Marge for the walk over to the Fat Cow.

"SOMEONE REALLY NEEDS to open up another diner here in town. This place is way too crowded," Marge said as she and Charlene stood in line at the cash register to pay for their coffee.

"It's not that bad." At least Mason wasn't anywhere in sight and he was the only person Charlene was in no hurry to run into. Not after last night.

Especially after last night.

That was the reason she'd called this morning and left a message with Lurline telling Mason that she couldn't make their scheduled lunch consultation. Not that they needed to consult on hairstyles anymore since they'd done so last night. She just didn't want him thinking they were still meeting today to go over the next topic—makeup. She needed a breather to get her head together and get herself back on track with her transformation.

Maybe tomorrow. Or the day after.

Better yet, maybe she would just finish the transformation by herself.

"Three coffees," she told the waitress when she stepped up to the register, Marge beside her.

"And a piece of chocolate cake," Marge added. "I'm not getting stuck caffeine free again."

The waitress retrieved a large slice, placed it in a white to-go container and handed it over to Marge before pouring three foam cups full of steaming black liquid. She slid the cups across the counter top and took the money Charlene handed her.

Grabbing her coffees and a few extra packets of sugar, Charlene turned to leave. She was just shy of the front door when she saw Skeeter McBee out of the corner of one eye and something that looked dangerously close to a wave.

A wave?

She turned just in time to see him wink and a lump jumped into her throat.

A wave *and* a wink?

Her throat burned and her stomach pitched. In all the time she'd been coming to the Fat Cow and Skeeter had been playing dominoes and gossiping at his usual table, he'd never once acknowledged her, much less waved or winked.

Because Skeeter paid no nevermind to the normal, boring folks of town. The only people he acknowledged were the ones he and his buddies talked about.

A smile followed the wink and her insides turned cold.

He knew.

The truth crystallized as her mind raced back through the past night's events. Mason's truck parked in front of her house. The cookies and the front porch swing. The orgasm on the swing.

Someone had seen them. That was the only explanation. Maybe someone had been out walking their dog or a car had passed by, or more likely, Janice Owens had been using her night vision binoculars. Regardless, someone had seen something and now the entire town probably thought that she and Mason had had wild, heathen sex in full view of anybody who might have happened by

The thing was, they hadn't actually done it. Sure, she'd had an orgasm. One of the best of her life. But as a result of little more than heavy-duty petting by today's standards. She hadn't stripped bare and he hadn't stripped bare, and they hadn't actually "climbed into the saddle" and gone at it.

The phrase reminded her of the book she'd hidden in her bottom desk drawer and Mason's words echoed in her head.

"When are you going to stop reading about life and start living it?"

The realization hit her as she stood there, the object of several pairs of knowing eyes. All of them attached to a bunch of old gossips who thought they knew what she'd been up to.

If only.

The minute the thought struck, she knew Mason was right about her. She spent her time reading about life rather than living it. She planned and contemplated and fantasized, but she never actually *did* anything. She never acted on half of what she felt inside.

She'd never had to. The planning and contemplating and fantasizing had always been enough to satisfy her.

Until now.

Until Mason McGraw had come back to town, back into her life, and given her a sample of the real thing.

And now the fantasies just weren't good enough. She wanted more. She wanted him.

She knew what she should do—finish the transformation on her own and steer clear of any and all temptation.

At the same time, she knew what she wanted to do. Right now. Right this moment.

She wasn't sure what happened to her in that next instant, but suddenly her misgivings faded. Maybe as a result of the morning's caffeine deprivation or the lack of sleep last night. Or maybe, just maybe, she was simply tired of fighting the need that pulled inside of her. Regardless, Charlene was through imagining what things might be like.

For once, she wanted to see for herself. She wanted to *live*. To lust.

For a little while, anyway.

The overwhelming desire burning her up from the inside out didn't change the fact that she wanted a happily ever after and she wanted it with a man who was more her equal than her opposite. After all, it took more than lust to build a solid relationship.

But to live out a fantasy?

Lust was plenty enough for that.

MASON HAD JUST stepped out of the shower after a grueling afternoon riding fence when he heard the knock on the front door.

He tried to ignore the sound as he reached for a towel. His muscles ached as he wiped at the water drip-dropping down his face. It was one of his hired hands, he knew. They usually knocked a few times before walking inside to take care of whatever business had brought them up to the main house.

It sure as hell wasn't a visitor. The Iron Horse sat a good forty miles outside of town, which meant that visitors were few and far between, and he certainly wasn't expecting anyone.

The knocking continued.

Okay, so it was probably one of the newer hands who didn't feel comfortable just waltzing in.

He ducked his head out the bathroom door. "Could someone get that?" he called out, a request that fell on deaf ears. Eustess and Lurline were too busy going at it over a blaring television in the back room.

Wrapping the towel around his waist, Mason left the bathroom and walked down the hallway toward the front door. He could wait for Rance to hobble in from the den, but that would take a few minutes since he still wasn't used to the crutches. And whoever was knocking didn't sound the least bit patient.

Knock, knock, knock, knock—

"The door's open," he growled as he grabbed the doorknob and hauled the thick wood toward him. "The door's *always* open…" His voice faded and all thought careened to a dangerous halt as his gaze drank in the woman standing on his doorstep.

"I'm ready," Charlene announced, looking like his hottest fantasy come to life.

His nerves prickled. There was something different about her. Something other than the come-and-get-me way she was dressed.

She wore the camouflage tank top he'd picked off the rack at Miss Jolie's boutique and a fitted blue-jean miniskirt that accented her round ass and revealed smooth, bare legs that seemed to go on forever before disappearing into a pair of tan cowboy boots that matched one of the colors in her top.

Her soft, pale hair hung loose and flowed down past her shoulders. She'd framed her eyes with a pencil liner that made them look even deeper and more sultry. Her plump red lips curved into a smile that stalled his heart for several long seconds.

"I guess I should have called first." He watched as she drank in his appearance and her smile widened. His heart gave a flip. "Did I catch you at a bad time?"

"A bad time for what?" he said, managing to find his voice.

"Our consultation."

"You cancelled," he accused, remembering the message Lurline had given him. *"I'm tied up and can't make lunch."* In other words, she'd been freaked out about last night and hadn't wanted to see him.

While he'd expected it, it had bothered him anyway. A hell of a lot considering that he'd wanted to see her in the worst way.

"I'm here to reschedule," she told him.

"For when?"

"Now. I had a makeup lesson at the Hair Saloon today, so I'm done with the appearance part of the transformation. That brings us to the second part—the moves. Since we never actually made it inside Wild West, I thought maybe we could take a drive out there tonight and see a few daring divas in action."

"You can see that at the nearest honky tonk."

"True, but they won't be professionals. I'd really like to see the pros in action. Besides—" she smiled and her eyes twinkled "—I've always wanted to see the place from the inside and I got all dressed up just for the occasion."

His gaze swept her again. "Nice boots," he finally told her when he met her stare.

"Thanks." Her smile faded and her eyes gleamed. "I bought them today. For tonight."

Yep, she was different, all right.

She had a confidence about her now that put his entire body on high alert and sent a rush of excitement through him. And if her sudden appearance hadn't been enough to stir him up, she reached out and topped it off with a soft, purposeful touch.

"You look good all wet." She traced a winding path of moisture down his slick stomach to where it disappeared into the towel knotted at his waist. "So," she said as she let her hand fall away after a seemingly endless moment. "Are you up for tonight?"

He grinned, his moodiness and exhaustion fading in a wave of anticipation. He was up, all right.

Boy, was he ever.

WILD WEST WAS everything Charlene thought it would be and more. The music was loud, the men were rowdy and the girls were beautiful. The only thing that turned out to be completely different from what she envisioned was Mason himself.

He was a man with a reputation for enjoying beautiful women and so she'd expected him to kick back and enjoy the show.

He didn't.

He sat up straight, his body tense, his gaze dark and hot and fixated on Charlene.

Despite all the eye candy surrounding him, from the waitress to the curvaceous woman prancing on the stage in front of them, wearing nothing but a neon pink g-string, a matching cowboy hat and a smile.

He didn't spare them a glance and the realization fueled Charlene's newfound confidence. So when the evening drew to a close and he started to take her home, she stopped him.

They ended up on a back road that led to a small creek that had once been the hottest make-out spot in town. Times had changed and the kids now hung out in a field near Simpson's pond. But that didn't dampen Charlene's excitement when she found herself sitting next to Mason on the tailgate of his truck. He'd pulled a sleeping bag from the cab and spread it out on the bed of the truck.

"I like a man who comes prepared," she told him as she settled next to him.

He grinned. "You can never tell when you'll get caught out in a storm and have to set up camp for the night. I was out rounding up cattle on this ranch in New Mexico one time and a storm hit so hard and so fast, that I ended up huddled in the cab of my truck in freezing weather, without so much as a blanket.

Never again. I've got a day's supply of food rations and a water bottle stashed, too. Just in case."

"I can't imagine what it would be like to sleep in my car."

"You do what you have to."

"But you don't have to do it," she replied. "You can hire people to run the ranch and do something else if you want to. Didn't you ever want to be a cop or a lawyer or a firefighter, or any of the other stuff most boys dream about?"

He shrugged. "Ranching's in my blood. It's who I am. Besides, I like it. I like it a lot." He stared up at the sky. "There's nothing like being on the back of a horse. The fresh air. The outdoors."

"The heat," she reminded him, thinking of the ninety plus weather they'd been having every day for the past two months. While the nights were bearable, cool even like now, the days were miserable.

"The heat can be something else. But I still wouldn't trade being outside for anything. Besides, you can always run the horse faster, which stirs a pretty decent wind." When she nodded, he added, "You've never been on a horse, have you?"

"Once. It was a pony, actually, and I was six years old. It was Tracy Smith's birthday party."

"The girl with the red hair and pigtails?" At her nod, he added, "I think I was at that party."

"You were. You and your brothers. The three of you threw spitwads at her dad's BMW."

He nodded. "That's right."

"You threw the farthest, by the way."

He looked surprised. "You noticed?"

"I always noticed."

Why-oh-why had she said that?

Because she'd thought it, and she was through with just thinking. Tonight, she was doing.

Silence stretched between them, the radio playing in the background.

"I noticed you, too," he finally said.

"Yeah, right."

His grin was slow and sure. "And I'll never forget how cute you looked in your *Hee Haw* panties."

"I'd rather not think about that."

"I thought about it. I thought about it a lot. You and your *Hee Haw* panties. You without your *Hee Haw* panties." His gaze shifted to hers and she saw the sincerity in his eyes.

Warmth unfolded in her chest. "You never even talked to me," she reminded him.

"I was a kid." He shrugged. "A sixth grade boy at the time. I didn't understand what I was feeling. And later when I did, I couldn't act on it. My parents had just died and I didn't need anything pulling me home when my grandfather was pushing me so hard to leave."

He looked so sad all of sudden, that she couldn't help herself. She reached out and touched his thigh, eager to chase away the hurt clouding his expression.

"I never had a chance to tell you how sorry I was about your parents. It was such a tragedy."

His hand closed over hers, his fingers warm and strong as he held her hand for a long moment. "Thanks, but it's okay now. Everything's okay. I'm home." His gaze caught and held hers. "With you." Before she could ask what he meant, he released her hand, his gaze shifting back to the creek. "So what happened with the pony?"

"I fell off and bruised my leg. I cried all the way home."

"I've fallen off a time or two. Or three. Or four. Or fifty-six."

"You've fallen off a horse *fifty-six* times?"

He nodded. "Most of that was back in my rodeo days. I was a bronc buster, so falling off went with the territory."

"I've seen *Urban Cowboy* twenty-eight times."

He cocked an eyebrow at her. "What does that have to do with bronc busting?"

"Watching John Travolta ride that mechanical bull is the closest I've ever come to seeing a real rodeo."

"You were born and raised in Romeo and you've never been out to the county fair?"

She shook her head. "I'm from the yuppie side of town, remember?" A strange sense of longing crept through her. "I always wanted to go. Back when I was a kid, my dad was always too busy with work and my mom was too busy running the house, so we never managed to make it out to the fairgrounds. In high school, I was always studying and none of my friends ever went, so neither did I."

"And now?"

She shrugged. "I've just never had the time."

"You have to go."

"Maybe I will." She realized what she'd just said and determination fired inside of her. *Maybe?* Tonight wasn't about *maybe.* It was about certainty.

It was about *doing.*

Starting right now.

12

CHARLENE SAT next to Mason and listened as Kenny Chesney's voice drifted from the radio. He sang about looking back and being young, reminding her of the past and the longing she'd felt for the man next to her. Fireflies danced over the rippling creek. The moon hung big and bright overhead.

It was a night she'd envisioned time and time again with Mason.

Almost.

She touched his arm.

"What is it?"

"Stand up."

He slid off the tailgate, a questioning look on his face as Charlene got to her feet and stood on the tailgate. She pushed the sleeping bag off to the side. Her ears tuned to the music and she closed her eyes for a long moment. The beat filled her head and thrummed through her body and she started to move.

She swayed, moving her hips from side to side. Sliding her arms into the air, she pushed her hands beneath her hair and lifted the silken weight the way she'd seen one of the girls do at Wild West.

The realization that Mason was there, waiting and watching her when he hadn't spared a glance for any other woman that night, made her heart pound even faster. Her blood raced and her movements grew more sultry.

All too soon, the song faded into a slow tune and she opened her eyes.

Mason stood on the ground and stared up at her, his eyes gleaming in the moonlit darkness. Tension held his body tight. His muscles bunched beneath his T-shirt. Taut lines carved his face, making him seem harsh, fierce, predatory.

Geez, her thoughts sounded like a cheesy romance novel. But what she felt—the intensity of her desire, the desperation—was the stuff of novels. And fantasies.

She'd felt just this way in her most erotic fantasy. Only Mason McGraw wasn't a figment of her imagination this time. He was real. He was here.

He wanted her.

She licked her lips before touching a finger to her throat, to the frantic pounding of her pulse. Her hand lingered before she slid a finger to the edge of her tank top, tracing the line where warm flesh met soft cotton before moving to the strap. Hooking her finger beneath, she slid the material down over her shoulder. Lifting her opposite arm, she did the same with the other strap until the material sagged around her shoulders. She shimmied a little and the tank top rode lower on her torso until the material caught on her bare, aroused nipples.

His Adam's apple bobbed as he swallowed.

A surge of feminine power went through her and she pushed the straps of her tank top down until the material hugged her waist. Grasping the top, she eased it over her hips until it puddled around her boots. Leaning down, she caught one strap and stepped free. Then with all the flourish of one of the Wild West dancers, she twirled the material over her head and tossed it to Mason.

He caught the top and dropped it to the ground, his attention never wavering from her.

Cool night air slid over her bare arms and breasts. Then his gaze chased away the sudden chill as quickly as it had come, heating her body, her blood, until she felt a bead of sweat glide down her temple.

She was hot.

A condition that had nothing to do with the heat wave sweeping through Texas, and everything to do with the fire that burned right here in this small part of it. Between herself and the man who anxiously waited for her next move.

She touched the undersides of her breasts, cupping the soft mounds, weighing them and feeling the heat of her own fingertips against the soft flesh. All the while, she imagined that it was Mason's touch that seared her. She skimmed her palms over her nipples and they throbbed in response. Her stomach quivered beneath her fingertips as she moved down. Past her belly button. To the snap on her blue jean miniskirt.

A few tugs and the opening slid free, her zipper parted and the material sagged. She rocked her hips in time to the slow, sweet, twangy song that filled the night air and the skirt slithered down her hips and legs. She bent her knee and stepped out of the denim before toeing it to the side with her boot.

She wore silk panty briefs much like the ones she'd worn when he'd walked in on her in the dressing room at Miss Jolie's. For a split second, doubt pushed past the passion fogging her senses. Her panties were a far cry from anything she'd seen the dancers wear at Wild West.

Why-oh-why hadn't she thought about new undies?

Because as bold as she was trying to be, this was all new to her. At heart, she wasn't a daring diva.

But Mason McGraw didn't seem to realize that. He stared at her as if she'd revealed a beaded thong, his gaze excited. Eager. Hungry.

The realization spurred her on and she trailed her fingertips over the satin of her panties. Desire speared her and she closed her eyes.

She teased the edge of elastic before pushing a finger past to slide along the damp, swollen flesh between her legs. She stroked herself and her nerves hummed. Another lingering stroke and she pushed deep inside her drenched flesh.

Pressure gripped her, so sweet and intense, and she gasped at the sensation.

She'd touched herself many times in this exact same way during any number of fantasies starring the hot, hunky cowboy standing at her feet. Yet, it had never felt the way it did now.

Another move of her fingers and her body swayed from the pleasure rippling along her nerve endings. But it wasn't enough. Not nearly enough.

She didn't want her own touch this time. She wanted his.

Sliding her finger free of her panties, she hooked the edges and slid the material down her legs and free of her body.

Righting herself, she stood before him, her skin bathed in moonlight, her nipples hard and throbbing, her cleft wet and pulsing. She held out her panties, part invitation and part challenge.

He quickly accepted both.

He took the lingerie from her hand and shoved it into his pocket before bracing one hand on the tailgate and hoisting himself into the bed of the truck.

He faced her, his gaze burning over her as he looked his fill.

"You are so beautiful. Every sweet inch of you."

"So are you."

"You can't see every inch of me. I'm not naked."

"So get naked."

He reached for the hem of his T-shirt, pulled the white cotton over his head and dropped it at his feet.

Where Charlene had only imagined him in her fantasies, now she saw with her own eyes. Muscles carved his torso, from his bulging biceps and shoulders to the rippled plane of his abdomen. Dark, silky hair sprinkled his chest, narrowing to a tiny whorl of silk that disappeared beneath the waistband of his jeans.

Her gaze swept down to the prominent bulge beneath his zipper, but oddly enough, she didn't feel even a moment's hesitation the way she had in the past, on the rare occasions when she'd actually had sex. Twice with an on again, off again boyfriend back in college. Once during grad school with a TA for one of her psychology classes. A few times over the past ten years with various colleagues who'd come and gone in her life.

She'd spent far too many years fantasizing about Mason McGraw.

Tonight was about making memories.

Enough to see her through the rest of her life because she knew deep inside she would never meet another man who made her feel the way that Mason did.

Hot. Bothered. Beautiful.

She felt all three as she stared up at him and he stared down at her and a fire as big as Texas blazed between them.

He touched her nipples, just the soft rasp of his

palms, and pleasure bolted through her. His strokes were featherlight and reverent as he brought the sensitive peaks to a tingling, swollen awareness. Then he slid his hands under her breasts and grazed her rib cage as he moved to cup her buttocks.

The truck dipped and creaked beneath them as he lifted her. He pulled her legs around him, locking her ankles at the small of his back. Then he settled her firmly against the rock-hard length barely contained by his zipper.

She wrapped her arms around his neck and lost herself to the delicious friction as he rocked her. The coarse material of his jeans rasped against her sensitive flesh, and pleasure rushed through her, igniting every nerve ending until her body glowed from the feel of his.

A day's growth of beard rubbed against the tender flesh of her neck, the slope of her breasts, chafing her and stirring her sensitive skin. He arched her backward, drew one swollen nipple into his mouth and sucked her so hard she cried out from the intense pleasure.

Then he captured her lips in a kiss that sent her thoughts spinning. His tongue tangled with hers, delving and tasting until she could barely breathe.

The next few moments passed in a fast, furious blur until Charlene heard the disc jockey's familiar voice drifting from the radio as he paused the music for a commercial.

"Time for a break, folks. We'll be right back with the good stuff after a word from our sponsors."

The words echoed in her head and sent a surge of reality through her.

"Wait," she breathed when she managed to tear her mouth from his. "Not yet. Not like this." She unhooked her booted ankles from around his waist and he let her legs slide down on either side of him until she stood in the truck bed.

She reached for the sleeping bag and spent the next few heart-pounding moments unrolling the padding and spreading it out in the bed of the truck, all the while conscious of his gaze.

She'd been painfully aware of her less than perfect body her entire life.

Until tonight.

She wasn't sure if it was the moonlight that fed her courage and made her walk a little straighter, or the boots which arched her back and pushed her breasts out. Or if it was just the fact that she wanted him so badly, she no longer cared that she didn't have an ass like J. Lo or a chest like Pamela Anderson.

Maybe all three.

She only knew that she didn't feel half as self-conscious as she did hungry.

Dropping to her knees, she reached for his hand and tugged him down onto the cushioned fabric. She urged him backward and straddled him, her knees planted firmly on either side of him.

"Now," she told him. "Like this." Settling her wet heat over his groin, she splayed her fingers in the hair covering his chest, her touch tentative, exploratory as she followed the path that narrowed down his abdomen. She stopped just shy of his waistband, mesmerized by the feel of his rock-hard abs.

His eyes burned midnight fire, his muscles tight with raw energy. He balled his hands into fists at his sides and she knew it took everything he had not to cover her hand with his and urge her on.

But he knew she wanted to do this herself. She needed to do it, and so he didn't move beneath her exploration.

A gasp parted his lips when she leaned down and caught one of his nipples between her teeth. She nibbled and suckled until she felt his hands on her shoulders. His fingers burned into her as he pushed her up to a sitting position and stared into her eyes.

"Unzip me," he finally said, his voice ragged. "Please, Charlie."

The sound of her name on his lips galvanized her into action. The zipper hissed and he sprang hot and eager into her hands. She trailed her fingers over him, tracing the ripe, plumlike head of his penis. He jumped in her hands and a drop of pearly liquid beaded at the tip. She leaned down and closed her lips around the smooth ridge and lapped at his essence with her tongue.

His deep, throaty groan sent a surge of feminine power through her she'd never experienced before.

But then she'd never loved a man with her mouth like this. Never held him in her hands and stroked him.

In a way, just this—this holding and stroking and tasting—seemed more intimate than anything she'd ever experienced in her past.

Sex had always been about getting to the climax. There had been a couple of tender kisses, lots of groping in the dark to remove clothes, a few moments of heavy panting; and then it had been over.

Pleasant. But over.

But this... This was surely the way it was meant to be between a man and a woman.

The thought sent a burst of joy through her, followed by a rush of panic.

A man and woman *in lust,* she reminded herself as she leaned back and grasped the edges of his jeans and briefs.

He lifted his hips and she tugged the material down his legs, pausing only to pull off his boots before stripping him completely bare.

He leaned up on his elbows and gave her one of those slow, teasing grins that never failed to stop her heart. "You aren't riding bareback tonight, are you, sugar?" When she shook her head, he motioned to the pocket of his jeans.

Charlene pulled a condom free, tore open the foil packet and rolled it down his hard length.

And then she did what she'd been longing to do

all day since she'd read the first riding tip in her latest how-to book.

She climbed over him and sank down onto his hard, hot length, until flesh met flesh and her body closed around him.

She started to move then, rotating her hips, her inner muscles contracting, sucking at him as the pressure built inside of her.

When he grasped her buttocks, she thought he meant to slow her down.

Desperation glittered in his eyes and his voice was raw and husky. "You're so hot, Charlie. So wet. So goddamned perfect." His fingers sank into her flesh, urging her to ride him harder, faster.

He was eager and out of control from then on, as if he'd fantasized about this moment, as well.

As if he'd fantasized about her just as he'd said.

Then again, she knew Mason was a passionate man. He'd done this many times before, felt it many times before. There was nothing different about this moment. Nothing special about it.

Nothing special about her.

Charlene told herself that, but she couldn't make herself believe it. Not after he'd admitted the truth to her. And certainly not when he stared so deeply into her eyes, his gaze full of longing and desperation and awe.

Because he fantasized about her.

He *felt* for her.

More than lust?

As quick as the question registered, it faded into a wave of sensation as Mason tightened his pelvis and thrust upward at the same time that she pushed down.

He went deeper only to urge her back up and thrust again.

And again.

Until she couldn't take any more.

The next few moments were like being sucked over a waterfall. The sensation swept her up and pulled her to the edge until all of a sudden, she plunged over. Pleasure crashed over her, turning her this way and that, consuming her and sucking the oxygen from her lungs for a long, heart-stopping moment.

Mason followed her quickly. His fingers tightened on her bottom. The muscles in his arms bulged. His body went taut and a deep, husky moan rumbled from his throat.

She collapsed on top of him and his arms slid around her, holding tight.

Not too tight, mind you.

It wasn't as if he never meant to let her go. Charlene had no illusions about that. This was lust, pure and simple, and it would end.

She'd learned that a long time ago when she'd watched her father walk away without so much as a backward glance at her mother, and all because the lust had burned up. Fizzled.

It would end, all right.
But in the meantime…
Charlene closed her eyes and relished the sound of Mason's heart which beat in perfect sync with hers.

13

MASON TURNED OFF the highway onto the main road leading to the Iron Horse. While Charlene had shown up at his place earlier that evening, they'd had to drive back through town on their way to Wild West, and so they'd dropped her car off and taken his truck.

He'd dropped her off more than a half hour ago, but her scent still lingered in the truck of the cab and his nostrils flared. His hands tingled, remembering the soft feel of her skin. And his dick throbbed remembering the warm, wet heat of her body.

Lifting his hips, he fished her panties out of his pocket and rubbed the soft cotton against his cheek. Christ, she'd felt even better than he'd anticipated..

While they'd had incredible sex under the stars, he'd been ready for even more when he'd pulled up at her house.

But it had been late and tomorrow was a workday for both of them. Besides, he hadn't wanted to push. Charlene had opened up to him tonight and accepted the lust that burned between them. And she'd acted on it. So he'd merely given her a deep, lingering kiss—a promise of things to come—and said good-night.

At the same time, turning and walking away from her had been one of the hardest things he'd ever had to do. Even though he knew it was only temporarily, the notion of crawling into an empty bed bothered him.

He rested the panties on the seat next to him, his fingers lingering on the soft cotton as his mind rushed back to the moment when she'd tossed the undies to him.

She'd looked so beautiful standing there bathed in the moonlight. More than that, however, she'd looked intense. Determined. *Hungry.*

If he'd had any doubts that she wanted him as fiercely as he wanted her, they'd been erased in that one moment. And each and every one that had followed.

"We can't keep our hands off each other."

Tucker's words echoed in Mason's head and he smiled.

The expression died, however, when he saw Eustess Ketchum's familiar, powder-blue 1954 Chevy pick-up sitting off to the side of the road, its hood up.

Mason pulled up behind the old truck, left his lights blazing and crunched down the gravel shoulder until he reached the driver's window.

Rance sat with his back to the passenger's window, his cast stretched out on the seat in front of him and his good leg resting on the floor, a white take-out container in his hands.

He shoveled in a plastic forkful of cherry pie and winked at his brother.

Mason's gaze narrowed. "What the hell are you doing out here?"

Rance held up his fork. "Eating."

"It's two o'clock in the friggin' morning."

"I know that."

"You should be home resting that leg of yours."

"I know that, too."

"You'll never get that cast off if you don't take it easy."

"Look, bro, you're preaching to the choir." He motioned to the raised hood. "I'd planned on being home in bed by this time, but the damned thing overheated." He shook his head and licked his fork. "I could have sworn the damned gauge looked fine when I got in."

"The gauges don't work."

"Uncle Eustess said everything worked."

"Everything did work that last time he drove it."

"Which was?"

Mason glanced at his watch. "I'd say about ten years now."

"You're kidding me, right?"

"He didn't even drive it out here when they moved in with granddad. Said he didn't want to stress out his new transmission, and so he had it towed. Aunt Lurline said it was on account of his cataracts, that he couldn't see the road well enough to get the truck out here without wrapping it around a tree. He'll argue differently, mind you."

"No kidding." It was more a statement than a question and Mason smiled.

"They're driving you crazy, aren't they?"

"Crazy enough to borrow a set of keys for a standard truck when it's my left leg that's busted up and risk going into town for a chili burger with extra cheese when I know good and goddamned well that Deanie Codge could pop up at any moment. Don't get me wrong. Aunt Lurline can cook like nobody's business and the food here is great, but I needed a decent meal without all the fussing and cussing."

Mason noted the white bag and the other empty containers sitting on the floorboard. "You didn't eat there?"

"I sure as hell did. But I had one of the waitresses fix me up an extra care package to go. And it's a good thing I did, otherwise I'd be starving by now."

"How long have you been out here?"

"Since about ten minutes after you left."

"That was seven o'clock."

"Tell me about it. I barely got to the diner before they closed at eight." He shook his head. "Damned cast didn't want to cooperate on the gear changes."

"I'm not even going to ask how you managed it."

"Good, because I'm grouchy and hurting and all I want is to hobble into bed and forget all about tonight."

"Come on. We'll leave the truck here and I'll come back for it in the morning."

"Uncle Eustess isn't going to like that too much. I had to promise to refill the tank and bring it back without any dirt or bug droppings on the windshield. Not bringing it back at all is sure to get him riled."

"He's always riled. Come on." Mason opened the door and reached out a hand to help his brother slide across the seat and onto his good leg. He reached in, picked up the crutches that sat in the gun rack that ran across the back window and handed them to Rance.

"Don't forget my other pies," Rance said as he tucked the crutches beneath his arm and started for Mason's truck.

Mason closed the hood and walked back to lean across the driver's side. "How many did you get?" He reached for the two full bags that held stacks of small white foam boxes.

"One of every kind."

"They've got twenty-three flavors." Mason followed Rance to the Dualie.

"I know. The peach is still as good as ever. I liked the cherry, too. And the lemon meringue. And the key-lime. Oh, and I'd definitely sell my soul for another slice of the peanut butter cream. The rest I'll try later."

"Forget getting well. You're liable to get fat." Mason walked around and pulled open the passenger door. The height of the truck was too much for

Rance and so Mason helped hoist his brother into the seat. "Yep," Mason told him. "You're getting fat, all right."

"You wish. Then you'd have an edge over me when it comes to the ladies."

"Don't need one," Mason said as he handed Rance the bags and walked around to climb behind the wheel.

"I'd say you don't." Rance held up the undies Mason had left on the seat. "Still charming the women out of their panties, I see."

"Just one woman."

Rance let loose a low whistle and arched an eyebrow at his brother. "Your girlfriend?"

"Yes." Or she would be just as soon as Stewart saw the new Charlene next Sunday and took a hike in the opposite direction. Then she would give up her theory and realize that Mason had been right all along, and they would live lustily ever after.

In the meantime, he was going to buy himself some added insurance by helping Charlene make one hell of a convincing transformation.

IT WAS ALMOST four o'clock in the afternoon and he still hadn't called.

Charlene forced her gaze away from the clock for the umpteenth time and tried to ignore the disappointment that rushed through her. Had he been turned off last night?

Her mind rushed back to the striptease and then

fast-forwarded through all that had followed. All of the kissing and touching. The panting and groaning. Hers and his.

But what stood out in her mind more than anything was the kiss on her doorstep. She'd expected fierce and urgent after the night they'd had. Instead, it had been slow and so sweet she'd actually wanted to cry.

Then again, her toes had been aching something fierce after wearing those new cowboy boots and so she knew her silly reaction had undoubtedly been because she'd been so relieved at the prospect of soaking her tootsies in a nice, warm bath.

It wasn't like she'd actually been sorry to see him go.

She forced her attention back to the case file for the sheriff and concentrated on making her notes on the session they'd just finished. His last session. He'd brought in his gift for his wife, and Charlene had given him a huge smile, a thumbs-up and a discharge.

After dozens of years of marriage, and as many bad, thoughtless gifts, the man had finally gotten it right. He'd bought an ornate wooden picture frame that fit three 5x7 pictures, the words *I loved you yesterday, I love you today and I'll love you tomorrow* engraved across the top. The right slot held a black and white photo of them playing golf on their honeymoon. The middle picture depicted them sitting in a golf cart out at the Romeo Country Club. The third spot was blank, waiting for the *tomorrow* just as the engraving promised.

Love.

The word lingered in Charlene's head. They loved each other, all right. And why not? They'd had plenty to fall in love with. They both lived to golf. The sheriff had also told her they enjoyed playing bingo together and tending their vegetable garden. It only made sense that they would be attracted to each other, in love with each other. They were soul mates obviously.

What didn't make sense was her attraction to Mason.

Not that she needed to worry about it now. Obviously, the lust had already started to fizzle. Just as she'd predicted. Otherwise, he would have called her. Why, it was already four fifteen…

The thought trailed off as she caught herself glancing at the clock again. She shook her head, finished the last of her notes and opened her bottom drawer to retrieve a Closed File sticker. She'd just grabbed the box, when her gaze snagged on the latest addition to her how-to collection.

So much for actually putting the darned thing to use. She'd done her best rodeo queen imitation, boots and all, and Mason obviously hadn't been that impressed. So much for the whole physical attraction theory.

She slammed the drawer shut, straightened her desk and retrieved her briefcase.

"I'm done for the day," she told Marge as she walked past her desk.

Marge arched an eyebrow as if to say already?, but she didn't open her mouth. Thankfully. Charlene needed to go home, crawl into her sweats and eat herself into a Happy Camper cookie coma before she did something really stupid.

Like call Mason.

Or worse, cry.

She had absolutely no reason to cry. Her feet were on the mend.

Unlike her ego.

She ignored the last thought, walked out into the hot afternoon heat and straight into Mason McGraw.

"What are you doing here?" she blurted, trying to catch her breath after walking head on into so much hard muscle.

Mason didn't give her the chance.

His arms slid around her and he hauled her even closer. "Nice to see you, too, sugar." He planted a kiss on her lips that was slow, thorough, sweet.

"I'm sorry I didn't call," he said before she could voice the question that had nagged her all day. "Somebody drove a car through our back fence. Nobody got hurt, but the barbed wire got all ripped up. Naturally, one of the calves got caught in it, which made a bad situation that much worse."

As soon as he said the words, she noted the cut on his cheek. "It looks like you got caught in it, too."

He shrugged. "I had to cut the calf loose."

Something teased her nostrils and she eyed him. "You came straight over here, didn't you?"

"I smell that bad?"

"Not exactly bad. Just different." Her nose wrinkled. "Okay, so maybe bad is a better adjective."

"I'm surprised you noticed, what with you being from the yuppie side of town and all."

"I've driven close enough to the city limits to know what a cow smells like."

"A woman who gets around. I like that." His green eyes twinkled. "So what are you doing tonight?"

"What are you doing tonight?"

He grinned and her heart stalled. "Helping you with the transformation. You got the moves down pat, but I still think you need a little work on the attitude."

"And here I thought I pretty much aced that aspect."

There was just something about the way he looked at her that made her feel as wild and as beautiful and as daring as she'd always wanted to be. And while she knew it was just an illusion caused by the lust that burned so fiercely between them, she couldn't help but embrace the feeling and go with it.

For now.

"I felt like stripping and so I did," she continued. "I felt like turning my fantasy into reality and having sex with you, and I did."

"See, that's the thing. We lived out your fantasy last night. I thought we could live out mine tonight."

Her heart hammered. Not only at the prospect of feeling him around her, inside of her, but because he'd obviously been telling the truth last night. He had fantasized about her.

"Actually, I had plans. I was going to eat my way through a box of Happy Camper cookies." *And then OD on a little tetracycline, followed by a heavy-duty acne scrub.* She smiled. "I guess I could trade the Mint Cream Extremes for a fantasy. But it'll have to be a really good one."

He grinned and kissed her again. "Put on one of your new miniskirts and meet me out at my place in two hours." His lips grazed her ear as he murmured, "Minus your undies."

"You have been thinking about this."

"About you." He gave her another kiss and a wink before he turned toward his truck, which he'd parked at the curb. "And don't forget your boots."

"IF YOU THINK I'm getting on that horse, you're crazy." Charlene stood just outside the main barn at the Iron Horse ranch and stared up at the chestnut mare. "Forget it."

Mason tossed a southwestern print riding blanket over the mare's back. "We'll ride double. I promise you won't fall. And if you get any bruises from riding, I promise to kiss them all better."

"I bet."

He finished harnessing the animal, hooked his

foot in the stirrup and climbed onto the horse's back. He looked down at her and held out a hand. "Come on. Just hook your boot in the stirrup and I'll pull you up."

She stared at him a few seconds before she slipped her hand in his. "Okay, but I want to go slow. No galloping."

"No galloping," he vowed as he hauled her up in front of him. "At least not during the first five minutes."

"Very funny." She had to hike her skirt up high on her thighs in order to spread her legs wide enough to accommodate the horse.

"I'm serious." He gripped the reins and gave the horse a little *giddyup*.

They bolted forward and Charlene grabbed Mason's thighs to keep from teetering to the side.

"Easy," he murmured.

The horse kept moving, the muscles bunching and rippling and Charlene clutched him tighter.

"I don't think she heard you," she said over her shoulder.

"Not her. You." He held the reins with one hand, and moved the other to cover her fingers which dug into his blue-jean clad leg. "Relax." His touch was warm and strong and purposeful.

They rounded the barn and started for the open pasture up ahead. True to his word, Mason kept them at a steady walk for the first few minutes and Charlene eased her grip.

"This isn't so bad—whoaaaaa!" They pitched forward as he urged the horse to a gallop.

Her heart lodged in her throat for the first few moments. But soon, she grew used to the steady pace and her body relaxed. Her grip on his thighs loosened until her hands rested easy on him and she actually started to enjoy herself.

The wind whipped at her face, sneaking beneath the edge of her skirt to tease her bare bottom. She became acutely aware of the powerful thighs that framed hers, his chest a solid wall of muscle behind her.

"Why don't you take the reins?" The deep voice slid into her ears. Without waiting for a reply, he urged the leather straps into her hands and she found herself steering the horse. "Just remember to keep your grip firm, but not tight. And don't jerk. You'll scare her if you do that."

"What if I want to stop?"

"We're not stopping until we're done." She had the sneaking suspicion that he was talking about more than just the ride.

A few frantic heartbeats later, he touched her thigh and she knew she'd been right. His palm burned into her flesh and her grip faltered.

Mason's other hand closed over hers, urging her fingers tight around the leather until she had a proper grip again.

"Concentrate," he told her.

"You try concentrating without your panties."

Laughter rumbled in her ears and danced along her nerve endings. "I guess that would make it a little difficult."

"More like hot. Is your bottom supposed to burn like this?"

"You have to rise and fall with the horse. Feel the motion with your thighs and let it guide you."

She spent the next few minutes doing her best to tune into the horse. But the only thing she seemed aware of was the way Mason's hands splayed on her thighs, his hardness pressing into her bottom.

"I don't think I'm good at this."

"You're trying too hard," he told her. "Just feel the animal and think about something else. Think about this."

His fingers made lazy circles on the inside of her thigh and Charlene's insides tightened. The movement continued for an endless moment before he urged the animal a little faster. The horse picked up the pace even more and so did Mason. His fingers swept higher, his touch more intense as he moved beneath the edge of her skirt and higher until he was an inch shy of the moist heat between her legs.

"See," he murmured against her ear, his husky voice gliding over her nerve endings. "You're doing it. You're moving with the horse. Can you feel it?"

The only thing she felt was him. Surrounding her. Filling her senses. Her heart pounded and her nipples tingled and she could barely think, much less form a reply.

"Charlene, are you with me?"

Boy, was she ever, she realized when his thumb brushed her clitoris and sensation speared, hot and jagged, through her body.

She would have dropped the reins if Mason's hand hadn't been fastened around hers, guiding the horse when all rational thought flew south to the pulsing between her legs.

"You're so wet." His words were more of a groan as he swept a finger along her slick folds. "So hot and wet and..." His voice faded into the pounding of her heart and the buzz of excitement that filled her ears.

She tilted her head back, resting in the curve of his shoulder as she surrendered herself to the ecstasy beating at her sanity and let him take control, of the horse and her body.

He slid a finger deep inside her and the air bolted from her lungs. He moved with the horse and so did she, shifting just so, riding his fingers the way the two of them rode the animal.

Her body grew tight and hot. The pressure built with each stroke, every thrust, until a cry broke past her lips. Her climax hit her hard and fast, like a zap of lightning that shook her to the bone. Shudders racked her. The blood hummed in her ears.

The horse seemed to slow with her heartbeat, until they moved at a slow, easy walk. Charlene had never felt as relaxed as she did at that moment with Mason's arms around her, his heart beating a steady tempo against her back.

The sun was just starting to set as they topped a small ridge and found themselves overlooking an endless stretch of green pasture dotted with lush trees.

"It's pretty isn't it?"

"Very. Is this your favorite spot?"

"It used to be. Actually, this is the first time I've ridden over this way since I've been back. The last time I was here was the night before high school graduation. Me and my brothers rode over, watched the sun set and said our goodbyes. The next day we walked across the stage, got our diplomas and went our separate ways." His arm slid around her waist and held her. "I never really knew this place existed until I followed my parents out here once. They used to ride together every Sunday afternoon."

"That's nice."

"It was the only thing they ever did together."

"At least they had a common ground."

"A lot of good it did them." The hurt in his voice tugged at something inside of her and before she could stop herself, she heard her own voice.

"My parents didn't do much of anything together. My dad was always busy working and my mom took care of the house."

"They obviously did something together, sugar. You're here, aren't you?"

"That was just sex."

"You say that like it's a bad thing."

"Not bad, but not enough."

"That's where I think you're wrong, sugar. Come on." He slid off the horse and turned to pull her down into his arms.

"What are we doing?" she asked as she watched him pull a soft plaid blanket from the saddlebags he'd draped over the back of the horse.

"I think it's time we had that fantasy." He walked toward a gigantic patch of wildflowers and spread the blanket in the center.

She followed. "You mean what just happened on the horse wasn't it?"

"Not all of it." He grabbed her hand and hauled her into his arms. His mouth covered hers, his lips plundering in a kiss that sent a flood of moisture between her already damp thighs.

He urged her toward the blanket and followed her down. His hard body covered hers and his mouth blazed a trail from her collarbone, down to the V of her bluejean vest. His fingers made quick work of the buttons until he parted the material, unsnapped her bra and shoved aside the lacy cups. Then his hot tongue flicked her nipple and her moan split open the peaceful sunset.

He teased the ripe peak, licking her over and over. Soon his lips closed around her areola and he sucked her so long and hard and deep that she thought she would come apart right there in his arms.

Sliding his hands beneath her skirt, he pushed the material up and urged her legs apart. He ground his pelvis against her softness and she gasped.

She could feel him hard and throbbing beneath his jeans and the realization sent a surge of restlessness through her. She grasped at his waistband and tugged at the button.

It slid open and his zipper parted. He sprang hot and heavy into her hands. She stroked him from tip to root and caught his moan with her mouth. The next few moments passed in a dizzying blur as she worked his erection, squeezing and massaging until he groaned and stilled her movements.

"Wait." He leaned away from her long enough to work his jeans and briefs down his thighs. He fished a condom from his pocket and sheathed his erection in one deft motion. Sliding his hands beneath her buttocks, he gripped her tight and drew her toward him as he thrust inside. His entry was quick and deep and she nearly exploded at the first moment of contact.

Mason ground his teeth against the overwhelming heat that gripped his throbbing erection. Christ, she was hot. And tight. And juicy. He closed his eyes and drank in a deep draft of air, determined to gather his control.

But he had none left. He'd thought about her all night. And all day. And now she was here, beneath him, pulsing around him.

She lifted her hips, urging him deeper and he lost

it. He rode her hard, his arms braced on either side of her, fingers clutching the blanket as he plunged deeper, faster, until she grasped his shoulders and moaned again.

A rumble worked its way from deep in his chest as he buried himself fast and sure and deep one final time. He bucked, spilling himself while her insides clenched and unclenched around him.

He rolled to the side and stared up at the sky as his heart threatened to burst from his chest. He covered his eyes for a long moment and fought for his breath.

Once he'd calmed down long enough to drag some oxygen into his lungs, he leaned up on his elbow and stared down at her. Her eyes were closed, her face flushed. Her lips were pink and swollen from his kisses. Her vest and bra lay open, her creamy breasts tipped with rosy nipples. The skirt rode her waist, revealing a triangle of soft, blond silk. Her legs were long and slim, her calves shapely where they disappeared into the sexy cowboy boots.

Mason had pictured her like this so many times. He'd wanted her like this so many times. But nothing he'd cooked up in his imagination had been quite as good as the real thing.

The real thing, he could touch. Smell. *Feel.*

He reached out and traced one nipple.

Her eyelids fluttered open and she smiled up at him. "So that was the fantasy."

"Almost." He leaned over and plucked a red flower from the edge of the blanket. "Now it's done." He tucked the flower behind her ear.

She smiled and the picture she made burned into his memory. So vivid and powerful that it haunted him the rest of the night and made him all the more determined to prove her wrong.

Because Mason McGraw wasn't letting her go.

Not now.

Not ever.

14

THE NEXT FEW days passed in a passionate blur for Charlene as she and Mason took turns breathing life into their most erotic thoughts of each other. They had wild, slippery sex in her shower. Fast, furious sex in the driver's seat of his John Deere tractor. Slow, tender sex between her favorite lilac-colored sheets. Fun, playful sex skinny-dipping in the McGraw River.

She knew it would end all too soon once Stewart returned home tomorrow and she proved her theory.

But she still had twenty-four hours left.

Until then, she was living for the moment, and fulfilling her most erotic dreams with Mason McGraw.

She stifled a yawn, took a huge sip of her coffee and smiled at the elderly couple sitting on the couch across from her.

"So, Lurline," Charlene said, glancing at her notes. "How have things been going?"

"Perfect, Doc. Things between me and Eustess are downright perfect. Ain't that right, Eustess?"

"You're darned tootin'."

"That means yes," Lurline said.

Charlene smiled. "I figured as much. Now, tell me what you mean by perfect? Are you talking more? Are you doing more activities together?"

"Oh, we're talking up a storm. Ain't that right, Eustess?"

"You're darned tootin'."

"And just yesterday, Eustess offered to help me can pickles. Right, Eustess?" She nudged her husband.

"You're darned tootin'."

"Why, Eustess has always loved my pickles. He couldn't wait for canning season. I'd get them into the jars and he'd turn right around and open them back up."

"Really? So this is something you used to do together?"

"All the time. Ain't that right, Eustess?"

"You're darned tootin'."

"That's wonderful," Charlene said.

"And that ain't all, Doc. We've been doing all sorts of things together here lately. We're shucking peas and working out in the tomato garden again. We even went for a walk the other morning right at sun up, just like we used to 'afore the kids were born. It's just like the old days."

"This is really fantastic. Eustess—" she started to say, only to have the man cut her off.

"You're darned tootin'."

Lurline elbowed him. "She ain't asked you nothin' yet, you old coot."

"Oh."

"Go on," Lurline said after giving Eustess a stern look. "Ask him something."

"Are you enjoying the extra time you're spending with your wife?"

"You're darned tootin'."

"And the activities that you two are sharing? You're all right with those?"

"You're darned tootin'."

"See, Doc," Lurline said. "I told you. We're cured. You're a miracle worker."

"I haven't done anything. You've both obviously been working very hard. You worked your own miracle. You've backtracked in your relationship to rediscover the common ground that drew you together in the first place."

Lurline smiled. "Does this mean we don't have to come back?"

"Not unless you start arguing again."

"Not us, Doc. We wouldn't dream of starting up, would we, Eustess?"

"You're darned tootin'."

Lurline nudged her husband. "You're supposed to say no."

"You told me to agree—yowww!" He rubbed at his leg.

"Let me rephrase that," Lurline said. "We've stopped arguing for good, haven't we, Eustess?"

"You're darned tootin'," he grumbled, rubbing his thigh. "I think."

"I'll pick you up at eight," Mason told Charlene after he helped Lurline and Eustess out to his truck. He stood in her office looking as handsome as ever in a green button-down shirt, the sleeves rolled up to his elbows, and a pair of faded jeans. It was her first glimpse of him that morning because Eustess and Lurline had been her first appointment and they'd been waiting for her when she arrived at her office.

Late, of course. Thanks to Mason and last night's skinny-dipping adventure.

"Tonight's my turn," she reminded him. He smelled of horse and leather and early morning sunshine. Her nostrils flared. "I thought we could stay at my place and have a little food fun. Maybe some whipped cream and carefully placed cherries."

He slid his arms around her and pulled her close. "We'll do anything you want, sugar." He planted a quick kiss on her lips. "But there's someplace I want to take you first."

"Where?"

He grinned. "We're going to a rodeo. The Romeo County Fair & Rodeo isn't for another two months, but Cherryville is having theirs this weekend. The competition starts tonight."

Charlene's heart started to race as she remembered all the times she'd wanted to attend the local festivities and never been able to. She'd dreamed of what it would be like. The noise, the excitement, the cowboys. But she'd never experienced it firsthand.

Mason was about to change all of that.

Charlene smiled. She had a feeling this was going to be the best night of her life.

FRIDAY TURNED OUT to be the worst night of Charlene's life.

She sat at her desk early Saturday morning—she'd gone into the office to catch up on all of her case notes which had fallen behind because she'd been busy all week with Mason—and ate half a box of Happy Camper cookies.

But even the sweet, addictive Chocolate Chippers couldn't soothe the terrible truth.

The worst night, all right.

It had started out promising enough. They'd arrived at the fairgrounds, purchased a couple of sodas and a funnel cake, and made it to their seats just in time for the first event.

That's when Charlene had realized that the rodeo was nothing like she'd expected. It was too crowded and dusty and dangerous.

She'd taken one look at the man sitting atop the vicious bronc who'd shot out of the gate, and she'd pictured Mason, and her heart had all but stopped beating.

Because she liked him.

She'd realized it then, and it had put a whole new twist on things.

She wasn't supposed to like *him*. There was absolutely no basis for her to like him. They had nothing in common.

Just lust.

Just like her parents.

Charlene picked up the phone and dialed her mother's cell phone. She'd given up asking questions a long time ago, but she needed a reminder of why she shouldn't get attached to Mason. She needed it in the worst way.

"Hello?" The familiar voice carried over the line.

"Hey, Mom. How's everything going?"

"Wonderful, dear. Your aunt and I are at an RV park outside of Fort Lauderdale and the weather is absolutely beautiful."

"That's good." Charlene made a little more small talk about the weather, before she added, "You know, I talked to Dad a few weeks ago and he's getting nothing but rain up in Pennsylvania."

"Actually, I wouldn't know. I haven't talked to your father."

"Because you can't stand him."

"I never said I couldn't stand your father."

"You act like it. You won't talk about him."

"There's nothing to talk about."

"But there is. Your past relationship. The breakup. The div—"

"I've gotta go, dear," her mother cut in. "Your aunt's calling me. We're taking the bus to the beach."

"But—" Charlene stammered, but the line had already clicked.

So much for reassurance.

"Somebody had a bad night," Marge declared as she walked in, a stack of charts in one hand and a giant mug of steaming coffee in her other.

"What are you doing here?" Charlene asked her.

"The same thing you're doing here. Catching up. Then again, you don't look like you're doing much work at the moment. You're moping."

"I'm not moping."

"I know moping when I see it. I guess things aren't working out with you and that tall, dark dream of a man."

"No, things aren't working out. They're not supposed to work out."

"Come again?"

"He's not my type."

Marge seemed to think about that. "True, but I still don't see your point."

"We're total opposites. We have no common ground."

"You like each other, don't you?"

"That's beside the point."

"How's that?"

"I'm not supposed to like him. He's all wrong for me." She shook her head. "I'm not doing this. I'm not making the same mistake that my mother made by falling for the wrong man."

"The wrong man? Your father wasn't the wrong man for your mother. He was the right man, which was why he took one look at your mother and fell head over heels. And she did the same."

"That's lust."

"Lust, love, it all goes hand in hand. If ever there was a match made in heaven, it was that one."

"Hello? My parents are divorced."

"True, but that wasn't because they didn't have a good marriage. Your mother loved your father and she loved him."

"And then it faded. Because there was no common ground."

"Is that what you think happened?" When Charlene nodded, Marge gave her a disbelieving look and sank down into a nearby chair. "You really don't know the story behind it, do you?"

"Do you?"

"Are you kidding? I was your father's secretary for all the years he worked here. I know everything, and I can tell you right now that the divorce had nothing to do with a sour relationship. If anything, it was the depth of their feelings for each other that forced them into a divorce."

"I'm not following you."

"Most people get divorced to save themselves. They either want out of a bad marriage, or they want to get into something they think is better. It's all about number one. But for your mother and father, the divorce came about because they were each trying to spare the other more pain and embarrassment."

"I'm still not following you."

"Charlene, your father was a financial genius when it came to other people's money. But he wasn't nearly as good with his own. He liked to gamble."

The minute Marge said the words, a long-forgotten memory surfaced. She saw her father filling in his name for a football pool for the Super Bowl. Not once, but several times.

"It started small at first, with football pools and such. Your mother didn't really understand the appeal—to her it was like throwing away a dollar and she would never do that. But your father enjoyed it. Before long he was going to the dog tracks over in Karnes County every Friday afternoon. One day, he bet a little too much and he had to take out an unofficial loan to cover himself."

"Unofficial? You mean, he stole money."

Marge nodded. "But I know he intended to put the money back. He was just backed into a corner and he couldn't touch his own money without your mother knowing it. Your father wasn't a bad man. He was just weak. When the powers that be over at the Savings & Loan found out he was skimming funds to cover his debts, they threatened to press charges. He borrowed money from his family up north to cover what he owed and then he resigned. Your mother couldn't handle the prospect of your father without a job. She'd been so poor growing up and when she realized that he had a long road to haul before he could ever hold down another job, it put a strain on her mentally. He didn't want to hurt her, and so he decided to leave. She knew he needed help and that he couldn't get it here, and so she let him. Your father went up north where he had family who could help him through his rehabilitation, and your mother stayed here to raise you."

The truth crystallized and suddenly all the bits and pieces of her past finally made sense. Her father's sudden leaving. Her mother's quiet acceptance. "Their relationship *didn't* fizzle. It died out," she heard herself say, remembering Mason's words.

"If you want to know what I think, I don't think it died out at all. I think they still have a thing for each other."

"Sure they do. Neither one of them will say two words about the other."

"Exactly. They avoid the subject because it reminds them of what they once had. And what they lost. Speaking of which, I'm going to lose my noon hair appointment over at the Hair Saloon if I don't finish up these notes and get out of here."

"Why didn't you ever tell me any of this?" Charlene asked as Marge stood to head back into the outer office.

Marge shrugged. "You never asked."

The news haunted Charlene for the rest of the morning as she tried to finish up her work.

Her parents didn't hate each other. If anything, the more she thought about it, the more she felt that Marge was right. Maybe they did still have feelings for each other.

At the same time, they weren't together, which meant those feelings weren't enough to make for a solid, lasting relationship.

Because her theory was right. They had no common ground, no shared interests, no meeting of the minds.

And Charlene would prove it tomorrow night.

Until then, she was getting her priorities straight. The transformation was complete, which meant there was no reason for her to see Mason again.

It was over.

MASON FINISHED the last of his early-morning chores and headed inside the house on Sunday morning to use the telephone. Again.

Charlene was avoiding him. He'd had a hunch yesterday when she hadn't returned his call. When he'd shown up at her house, she'd made an excuse about not feeling well. But he knew something was different between them. Something had changed.

Over.

The word echoed in his head as he entered the house and headed down the hallway to the kitchen.

Over wasn't a possibility. They were too good together.

Eustess and Lurline were arguing over a piece of bacon when he walked into the room. They took one look at him and the arguing stopped.

He turned his attention to Rance who sat at the kitchen table, his cast propped on a chair, the phone pressed to his ear.

"Come on," he was saying. "You have to do this."

"Get off," Mason told his younger brother. "I need to make a call."

"Just a sec. Listen, I really need this favor—" Rance's words came to a dead stop as Mason pressed the button on the wall unit and disconnected the call. "Hey, what did you do that for?"

"I need the phone. Now."

"Well, I needed it, too."

"Not more than me."

"Says you. Wilson Bingham saw me at the diner the other night and he told Morris Townsend, who told Jackie Donner, who told Marsha Rhinehart who just happens to be getting up close and personal with Clay Codge." He ran a hand over his face. "He's going to tell Deanie and she's going to be out here like a fly on a slice of cherry pie."

"Maybe she won't care."

"Yeah, right." He shook his head. "Christ, I'm screwed."

"Welcome to the club." Mason punched in Charlene's number, only to get her answering machine. Again. He left a message asking her to call him before sliding the receiver into place.

"Trouble with the girlfriend?"

"Maybe." He shook his head. The only trouble was that Charlene still thought she was right about her theory. But that would change soon enough tonight and they could get back to enjoying each other.

Tonight.

He held tight to the thought, handed his brother back the phone, then turned on his heel to go and take a shower. Tonight she would see for herself that physical attraction was everything. And Mason intended be there when she did.

"CHARLENE?" Stewart's amazed voice greeted her when she walked into the Steak-n-Bake on Sunday evening.

She wore a low-cut black dress that clung to her body like a second skin and three-inch heels. She'd spent four hours on her hair and makeup and she looked every bit the daring diva.

She gave him a wink and a smile. "Welcome home."

He frowned as she slid into the seat opposite him. "What happened to you?"

"What do you mean?"

"The way you're dressed... Your hair... All that makeup..." He shook his head. "What happened?"

"I had a little makeover. Do you like?" She did a suggestive lip lick and gave him her most sultry look.

"I, um, guess."

"You do?"

He shrugged. "If you like it, that's all that really matters. Listen, I'm glad you could meet me here because I really need to talk to you." He leveled a stare at her. "It's about us."

Here it comes, she thought. He was going to declare his devotion, prove her right and suggest they start seeing each other.

"I think we should stop seeing each other."

His words registered and she blinked. "What?"

"I mean, I know we're not really seeing each other right now, not romantically, that is, but I think we should stop seeing each other, period. It's just that I've met someone and she just doesn't understand the whole friendship thing."

He'd met someone. No doubt a fellow pediatrician from the conference. Someone even more perfect for him than Charlene.

"We've been seeing each other off and on for the past six months."

"*Six* months?"

"I wanted to tell you before, but I wasn't sure it was going to work out between us. And you're such a good friend that I didn't want to act prematurely and risk losing our friendship over something that might not work out. But then she went to the conference with me and I realized that I just can't live without her."

"That's great." Relief washed through her, followed by a strange sense of panic. Relief? She wasn't supposed to feel relieved. Her theory was dead in the water. All of the common ground that she was so sure made them perfect for each other faded in the face of Stewart's "I can't live without her."

"So, um, tell me about her. What does she do for a living? Where is she from?"

"She works here actually. She's the seating hostess." He pointed to the tall redhead that stood near the front door. She wore a short red dress that hugged her breasts and emphasized her long legs. Her hair was long and tousled, her makeup dark and sultry. "We met when she seated me for a business dinner. I asked you here tonight because I wanted you to meet her and I wanted her to meet you." His eyes took on a desperate light. "I was hoping you might reassure her that there's never been anything between you and me. That we're just friends." He lowered his voice a notch. "She's really jealous."

"I guess I could do that. So you're sure this is the woman for you?"

He nodded. "We have really great chemistry."

15

WHEN CHARLENE LEFT the Steak-n-Bake she found Mason waiting outside for her. It was late afternoon, the sun just an orange glow on the horizon. The restaurant had switched on their outside lights and there was no mistaking the look on Mason's face. He leaned one hip against her bumper, his arms folded, his gaze bright and twinkling and excited.

"What are you doing here?" she asked after she'd crunched across the gravel parking lot toward him.

"Moral support." He took a long, thorough look at her and appreciation glimmered in his gaze. "You look really great."

His words sent a zing of electricity up her spine. A feeling that quickly died, buried by the disappointment churning in her chest. Suddenly, she didn't just want Mason to like the way she looked. She wanted him to like her.

As much as she liked him.

"So how did it go?" He pushed away from the bumper and came up to her.

"You were right. My theory is total bunk." She

tilted her head back and stared up at him. "He told me that he found someone else."

"Really?" A dark, fierce light gleamed in his eyes in that next instant, as if he wanted to hit someone almost as much as he wanted to pull her into his arms. But then it disappeared and she was left to wonder if she'd only imagined it.

"The hostess with the mostest," Charlene continued. "She works here. They met when she seated him for some business dinner. Her name's Veronica and they've been seeing each other ever since. They have great chemistry."

"Veronica? Veronica Miles? Wasn't she the homecoming queen when we were freshmen?"

"That's her." One of the original daring divas. Stewart's complete opposite, not to mention his senior.

But none of that mattered.

"They have great chemistry."

"If that don't beat all." He shook his head as he reached for her. "Good for him." Pulling her into his arms, he added, "And even better for me. There's nothing wrong with two people being physically attracted to each other."

"I know that."

"It's a good start. A damned sight better than most." Meaning his parents. Meaning that he didn't put an ounce of importance in common interests or like personalities.

And neither did Charlene.

"You're right." Her words widened his smile. "First, it's physical attraction and before you know it, two people actually like each other."

"I do like you, Charlene." He gave her a sweet, lingering kiss that promised many more. "I like you a lot and I think we ought to do something about it."

"I agree." She nodded. "We should stop seeing each other."

"Exactly. We should get married and stop all this beating around the bush…" His voice trailing off as her words registered. *"What?"*

The word *married* lingered in her head and tears burned the backs of her eyes. It was hardly the proposal she'd always imagined. At the same time, it sent a rush of joy through her so fierce that it frightened her.

Because she not only liked Mason. She loved him. It made no sense, but she felt it anyway. The attraction. The emotion.

Love.

"I realize my theory isn't all it's cracked up to be," she blurted, eager to say something that didn't involve the word *yes!* "But couples with common ground *do* tend to run the greater chance of success. I've seen it professionally many times. I just finished a counseling session with the sheriff. He and his wife have been married forever and they've been playing golf together just as long. And then there's your aunt and uncle. They've had a long, healthy marriage and conquered their arguing because they rediscovered their own common ground." She latched on to the notion, desperate to ignore the urge to throw herself into his arms and never let go. She wouldn't, she couldn't.

Because while Charlene did, indeed, love Mason, he didn't love her. He liked her.

He liked an image.

When he looked at her, he didn't see below the surface. He saw the daring diva he'd spent the past few weeks helping to create.

He liked *her*, all right. The woman who'd stripped bare on the tailgate of his truck, who'd voiced her fantasies and pranced around in a pair of cowboy boots and nothing else.

An illusion.

While Charlene had done all of those things and truly enjoyed them, it had all been part of a test.

Deep down, she was still the same person he'd spent a lifetime ignoring.

"That's crap," he told her, his gaze narrowing.

She pulled her shoulders back and met his stare. "It's not crap. Your aunt and uncle are proof enough. I really have to go."

And then she pulled away from him, climbed into her car, started the engine and drove away.

It was for the best, she told herself as she glanced in the rearview mirror. He stood in the parking lot, staring after her, his face a dark mask, and her chest tightened.

She gripped the steering wheel and ignored the urge to turn the car around.

Once he saw through the surface to the real woman beneath, he wouldn't feel near the attraction he felt for her now. He wouldn't want her anymore, the relationship would end and she would hurt even more than she did right now.

Mason McGraw was all wrong for her.

She *knew* that.

At the same time, she couldn't help but feel that she was walking away from the best thing that had ever happened to her.

SHE WAS CRAZY and he was a damned sight better off without her.

That's what Mason told himself on the drive back to the Iron Horse. The thing was, he didn't believe a lick of it by the time he reached the ranch.

In the two weeks since Charlene had walked back into his life, he'd been happier than he'd been in a long, long time.

She not only reminded him of all the good things in his past—growing up and cutting loose—but she made him see all the good things he could have.

He wanted to make love to her every night, to fall asleep in her arms and wake up to her every morning.

And she didn't.

Because they had no common ground. Because they were opposites.

Because she believed that his aunt and uncle had conquered their arguing because they'd rediscovered their own common ground.

Right.

He stormed into the house and ran straight into Rance who stood on the other side of the doorway.

"It's you," his brother exclaimed. "You scared the shit out of me. I didn't expect you back so soon. When I heard the truck, I figured it was Deanie in her Dualie and—hey, where are you going?" he called after Mason who walked past him.

Straight to the den where Eustess and Lurline were busy arguing over the remote control.

The minute they spotted him, the bickering stopped.

"Why, dear, we didn't hear you come in," Lurline exclaimed, handing over the remote control to Eustess.

"It's no wonder with all the fighting goin' on in here."

"Why, we weren't fighting, dear. Not at all. Were we, Eustess?"

The old man spared a glance as he flipped the television channel from Lurline's favorite soap opera to a reality court show. "You're darned tootin'."

"You crazy fool." Lurline slapped him on the arm and snatched the remote control from him. "That means yes."

"I mean, you ain't darned tootin'. Gimme that."

"See? You're still arguing."

"This is just a little disagreement."

"I know you're still arguing. It's impossible not to know it. What I want to know is why Charlene thinks you've stopped."

"Because we told her so." Lurline drew a deep breath and pushed to her feet. "Dear, we tried to stop. We really did, but the thing is, we like to argue."

"Come again?"

"That's right, boy," Eustess added. "Ain't much else for us old folks to do. Going at it with your aunt gets my blood pumping and keeps me feeling young."

"Me, too." A wistful looked touched Lurline's face. "We used to do other things that were just as exciting, if you know what I mean." A blush colored her cheeks. "But then you get old and you can't do the things you used to. So you find other ways to stay in touch with each other."

"By arguing?"

"We don't exactly look at it as arguing. We talk to each other. It gets loud sometimes. And we disagree. But then that's the fun of it. Ain't that right, Eustess?"

"You're darned tootin'."

"What about you rediscovering common ground? You never had any common ground."

"Well, we sort of lied about that. We didn't want you to worry about us anymore and we knew Dr. Singer wouldn't give us a clean bill of health unless she thought we were communicatin' again, as she called it. So I sort of told her that Eustess was helping me can pickles. And that we were gardening. And I may have thrown in a little bitty lie about us taking walks together in the morning like we used to do before the kids were born."

"Uncle Eustess used to feed a ranch full of horses every morning."

"We know that, but she doesn't."

He gave them both a stern look. "She's about to find out. Come on."

CHARLENE HAD JUST slathered an acne scrub onto her face when she heard the doorbell ring. She wiped the tears from her eyes—she'd been crying ever since she'd walked into the empty house and straight into her comfort sweats.

But the soft, warm cotton hadn't made her feel any better. She still felt cold. And alone. And miserable.

Even half a box of Happy Camper cookies hadn't helped. And now she was out, and in desperate need of a fix. She'd left a message for Janice asking for another case.

Unfortunately, she had the feeling that wouldn't be near enough to help her get over Mason.

"I'm coming," she called out as she reached the bottom of the staircase. "Thanks so much for coming—" The words caught in the sudden lump in her throat as she found Mason standing on her doorstep, flanked by Eustess and Lurline.

"What are you doing here?"

"Tell her," Mason instructed.

"We lied," Lurline blurted. "We're still fighting. Ain't that right, Eustess? And forget the darned tootin'. Just say what's on your mind."

"Wasn't my idea to lie. Lurline cooked that up."

"Why, you old coot. I'm not taking the fall for this all by myself. You're just as responsible as I am."

"I ain't got a deceitful bone in my body."

"And I ain't got a gray hair on my head." Lurline frowned at him before turning to Charlene. "We're sorry. It's just that we knew our arguing was bothering Mason, but we couldn't stop. We tried. So we figured if we convinced you, you would convince him and he would stop worrying over us. But then he heard us at the house."

"On account of you got a big mouth," Eustess told his wife."

"No bigger than yours…" Their voices faded into a string of bickering as Mason stepped forward.

"They lied to you. They're still arguing."

"And the pickle canning?"

"Uncle Eustess is allergic to pickles. It was all a lie. They like arguing."

"You're kidding, right?"

Mason turned to his aunt and uncle. "Time out," he said, his voice so loud that it cut them both off midsentence. He gave them another stern look. "Tell her the rest."

"We never really have done a lot together. But we do talk. Or we used to. Then as we got older, the talks got louder on account of neither of us can hear all that well. And then we sort of started disagreeing a lot. Eustess used to do it to pick at me at first. He knew it got me riled up and he liked to see me like that."

"Ain't nothin' prettier than a woman with a flush to her cheeks," the old man remarked.

"They like arguing," Mason told her. "It's how they stay connected. Excited. It's their passion. So you see? They aren't proof of anything, except the older you get, the crazier you get. You and I...we can work."

She shook her head. "There is no we. There's you and who you think I am. But the boots and the miniskirts and the hair... That's not the real me. You don't know the real me."

"You mean the real you who walks around in sweats and wears white scrub all over her face?"

The minute he said the words, she had the sudden urge to turn and race back up the stairs, snatch up the nearest miniskirt and wash her face.

She forced her feet to stay rooted to the spot.

"This is me," she said. "I have really bad skin without this stuff. And I have four pairs of old sweats as ratty and worn as these, and I wear them every night. They're comfortable. They're me."

"They're sexy."

"They're not. I'm not. The woman you went out with wasn't the real me. I was pretending."

"Sugar, you weren't pretending. You were cutting loose, opening up. That was the real you. And so is this. It's all part of the same package."

"My favorite part of the rodeo was the funnel cake."

"I've got an affection for funnel cakes, myself. So see, we're not totally without common ground."

"It takes more than lust to make a relationship work."

"I know that. It takes a little bit of everything. A little lust. A little common ground. A lot of love—"

"What did you say?"

He leveled a gaze at her. "That it takes love."

"I didn't think you believed in love."

"I didn't. Until I met you. You made me feel things…" He shook his head, as if searching for the right words. "Things I've never felt before. I wanted to get inside of your sweet body so bad, but along the way, I found myself wanting to get inside your head, as well. I didn't just want to make love to you. I wanted to talk to you, spend time with you. I like seeing you smile. I love you, Charlene." His gaze roamed over her face and she saw the glimmer of emotion in his eyes. "I love all of you, though I'd prefer it if you didn't come to bed every night with all this stuff on your face. Not because you look bad," he added when she bristled. "But because I like to touch you. You have soft skin."

"Really?"

"Really. You're beautiful. You've always been beautiful, even in the *Hee Haw* panties."

"Even like this?"

"Even like this." He pulled her into his arms and kissed her. When he broke away, he had an acne cream mustache.

Oddly enough, it didn't take away from his good looks. Because Charlene saw past the surface to the man beneath. The man who stared at her with such love and longing in his gaze that her heart swelled.

"I love you," she told him. "I always have."

"Good, because I don't intend to let you go. You're marrying me, and if you try to run, I'll hunt you down and hog-tie you."

She eyed him. "Is that a promise?"

"I thought the daring diva was just an act."

She shrugged. "It was, but it was also fun. Besides, it was hard enough breaking in those boots. I'm not giving them up after all that work. And I've got a few fantasies we still haven't tried."

He grinned. "I've got a hell of a lot more than a few. Enough to keep us busy for a long, long time."

"For forever?"

"Forever," he promised. And then he kissed her.

Epilogue

"HIDE ME," Rance said as he rushed into the makeshift dressing room set up in the back of the Romeo First Presbyterian Church where Mason and Josh were busy changing into their tuxedos. His heart hammered and he swallowed the sudden rush of panic that rose in him as he slammed the door. "She's here," he announced.

"Who?" Josh paused tying his tie to glance over his shoulder.

"*Who?* Deanie, that's who. Deanie Codge. I saw her truck pull up outside." Rance shook his head, the image of her navy blue 4x4 crawling through the parking lot still vivid in his mind. "I knew she would come running as soon as she caught wind that I was back."

"You've been home for two months," Mason reminded him as he finished his own tie and reached for his jacket. "The whole town knows you've been home since you went to the Fat Cow diner on that chili burger mission. I'd say she caught wind long before now."

Rance had had the same thought, but obviously he'd been wrong. No way would Deanie have stayed away if she'd known.

The woman didn't know how to stay away.

"Yeah, well, maybe she's been busy or sick or maybe she's just been biding her time. It doesn't matter. The fact is, she's *here*."

Finally.

The word whispered through his head and he pushed it back out. It wasn't like he cared that she was here, or that he'd thought for a little while that he might actually be losing his touch when it came to women. Deanie had worshiped him, for Christ's sake.

And she obviously still did.

"Would you just calm down," Josh told him as he slipped on his own jacket. "She's here because the whole damned town is here. Between Holly and Charlene, they've invited practically everyone."

He frowned. "That's just what she wants everyone to think. She's obviously got something up her sleeve. She's trying to catch me off guard. Maybe slip something in my drink when I'm not looking at the reception so she can haul me home and have her way with me."

Mason grinned. "I think you've been spending too much time with Eustess and Lurline. All the arguing is warping your brain."

"My brain is just fine. I can't believe you guys aren't worried. You know how she used to be." He rubbed his suddenly damp palms on his pants. "This would have to happen to me. It's not enough that I had to break my leg. Now Deanie's tracked me down."

"Why don't you look at this as an opportunity?"

Mason clapped his younger brother on the back and steered him out the door and down the hall. Josh followed.

"It's been a long time," Mason told Rance as they lingered in the hallway outside the sanctuary. Inside, the sound of an acoustic guitar greeted the guests. "Maybe things between you two have changed."

"I doubt that. The woman is crazy about me."

"Really?"

"She can't get enough of me."

"Is that so?"

"She's hooked."

Mason pointed past him. "She's right behind you."

Rance whirled in time to see Deanie Codge exit the ladies' room and come to a dead stop, her gaze hooked on him. She looked exactly the same as she had all those years ago, with her long, dark hair and her bright blue eyes. Rance's entire body went on red alert.

He braced himself for a running tackle, but she simply smiled.

And then she walked the other way.

"Yeah, she's still hooked, all right," Mason said. "She obviously can't keep her hands off you."

"She can't." Rance watched her take the arm of an usher and disappear into the sanctuary without so much as a backward glance.

At least, at one time, she hadn't been able to keep her hands off him.

Things had obviously changed. Deanie Codge wasn't the same lovesick girl she'd been when they'd been kids. She was all grown-up now.

And she wasn't the least bit affected by Rance, it seemed.

It's about time. Even as the thought rolled through his head, he didn't feel nearly the relief he should have.

"It's time." The announcement came from the minister who joined the three men, urging them down the hall and through a door that opened at the front of the sanctuary.

Rance took his place as best man, pasted on a wide smile and did his best to concentrate on his brothers and the ceremony taking place, rather than the woman who sat five pews away, her gaze anywhere, everywhere, but on him.

She'd changed, all right, and damned if it didn't bother Rance a hell of a lot more than it should have.

Enough that he made up his mind then and there, that he was going to find out why. Even if it meant that he'd be the one doing the chasing. He sort of liked the idea of turning the tables on her.

If Deanie thought she'd been persistent all those years ago, she hadn't seen anything yet.

* * * * *

Rance will finally get his girl...
but he'll have to work for her.
Watch for the fireworks next January in
Tall, Tanned & Texan.

MILLS & BOON®
Live the emotion

Blaze™

RED LETTER NIGHTS
by Alison Kent, Karen Anders and Jeanie London

A red-hot secret love note gets the holidays off to a passionate start for three single girls – Claire, Chloe and Josie – and soon all of them are experiencing all kinds of pleasure in the company of three very sexy men.

POSSESSION *by Tori Carrington*
Dangerous Liaisons, Bk 1

When FBI agent Akela Brooks returns home to New Orleans, she never expects to end up as a hostage of Claude Lafitte – or to enjoy her captivity so much. She immediately knows the sexy Cajun is innocent, but for Akela, that doesn't make him any less dangerous…

MAJOR ATTRACTION *by Julie Miller*

Popular Dr Cyn's latest advice column is sending military men running for cover – except Major Ethan McCormick. But after one sexual encounter with Ethan, she's willing to concede a major attraction – especially when he's *out* of uniform!

ROCK MY WORLD *by Cindi Myers*

A three-day bed-in publicity stunt with the gorgeous Adam Hawkins? Erica Gibson could hardly believe her luck! After the lights go out, Erica breaks all the rules and seduces him. Back at work, they try to forget their nights together, but there's nothing like forbidden passion…

On sale 6th October 2006

Available at WHSmith, Tesco, ASDA, Borders, Eason, Sainsbury's and most bookshops

www.millsandboon.co.uk

MILLS & BOON®
Live the emotion

Modern
romance™
Extra

Two longer and more passionate stories every month

MARRIED IN A RUSH by *Julie Cohen*

One look from handsome stranger Bruno Deluca and Jo Graham's resolve melts. It's not as if carefree summer-loving with a tall, gorgeous man is meant to lead to a life-long commitment – Jo doesn't do commitment…not with anyone! But now she's pregnant, and sexy Bruno wants to marry her – whether she likes it or not!

SEEING STARS by *Kate Hardy*

Though Adam McRae is sexy enough to create X-rated visions for pyrotechnician Kerry Francis, they are just friends. Until Adam asks her to be his fake fiancée…and they end up getting hitched! A wedding night to remember follows – but now Kerry's in love, what happens once the (fake) honeymoon is over?

On sale 6th October 2006

Available at WHSmith, Tesco, ASDA, Borders, Eason, Sainsbury's and most bookshops

www.millsandboon.co.uk

0806/055/MB044

Sexy!

Three steamy, sultry reads to get the temperature rising this autumn

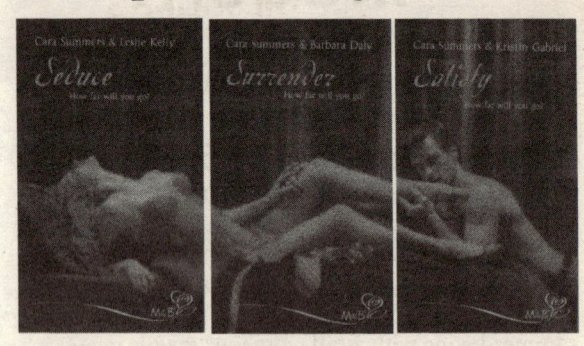

Seduce

The Proposition by Cara Summers &
Wickedly Hot by Leslie Kelly

Available 21st July 2006

Surrender

The Dare by Cara Summers &
Kiss & Run by Barbara Daly

Available 18th August 2006

Satisfy

The Favour by Cara Summers &
Good Night, Gracie by Kristin Gabriel

Available 15th September 2006

www.millsandboon.co.uk

Seductive, Passionate, Romantic
There's nothing as sexy as a Sheikh!

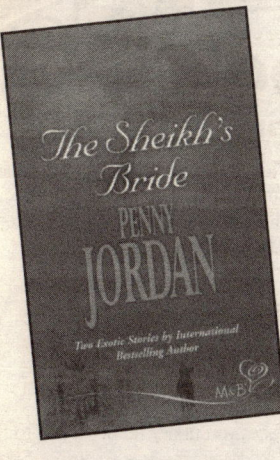

THE SHEIKH'S BRIDE

Featuring *The Sheikh's Virgin Bride* and *One Night with the Sheikh* by Penny Jordan

Available 1st September 2006

THE SHEIKH'S WOMAN

Featuring *The Arabian Mistress* by Lynne Graham and *The Sheikh's Wife* by Jane Porter

Available 15th September 2006

Collect both exotic books!

www.millsandboon.co.uk

FREE!

2 Books
and a surprise gift!

We would like to take this opportunity to thank you for reading this Mills & Boon® book by offering you the chance to take TWO more specially selected titles from the Blaze™ series absolutely FREE! We're also making this offer to introduce you to the benefits of the Mills & Boon® Reader Service™—

- ★ FREE home delivery
- ★ FREE gifts and competitions
- ★ FREE monthly Newsletter
- ★ Exclusive Reader Service offers
- ★ Books available before they're in the shops

Accepting these FREE books and gift places you under no obligation to buy, you may cancel at any time, even after receiving your free shipment. Simply complete your details below and return the entire page to the address below. You don't even need a stamp!

YES! Please send me 2 free Blaze books and a surprise gift. I understand that unless you hear from me, I will receive 4 superb new titles every month for just £3.10 each, postage and packing free. I am under no obligation to purchase any books and may cancel my subscription at any time. The free books and gift will be mine to keep in any case.

K6ZEF

Ms/Mrs/Miss/Mr .... Initials ....
Surname .... **BLOCK CAPITALS PLEASE**
Address ....
....
.... Postcode ....

Send this whole page to:
UK: FREEPOST CN81, Croydon, CR9 3WZ

Offer valid in UK only and is not available to current Mills & Boon® Reader Service™ subscribers to this series. Overseas and Eire please write for details. We reserve the right to refuse an application and applicants must be aged 18 years or over. Only one application per household. Terms and prices subject to change without notice. Offer expires 31st December 2006. As a result of this application, you may receive offers from Harlequin Mills & Boon and other carefully selected companies. If you would prefer not to share in this opportunity please write to The Data Manager, PO Box 676, Richmond, TW9 1WU.

Mills & Boon® is a registered trademark owned by Harlequin Mills & Boon Limited.
Blaze™ is being used as a trademark. The Mills & Boon® Reader Service™ is being used as a trademark.